THE WAND THAT ROCKS THE CRADLE

STORIES OF MAGICAL FAMILY

MISHA BURNETT   MARION DEEDS

W.O. HEMSATH   JOANNA MICHAL HOYT

MICHELLE F GODDARD   ELANA GOMEL

FRANK SAVERIO   P.L. SUNDESON

Edited by
OREN LITWIN

LAGRANGE BOOKS

ALSO EDITED BY OREN LITWIN

Liberty Island Media

The Odds Are Against Us: An Anthology of Military Fiction

Lagrange Books

Ye Olde Magick Shoppe: Stories of Magic for Sale

Bad Dreams and Broken Hearts: The Case Files of Erik Rugar, by Misha Burnett
(coming soon!)

CONTENTS

INTRODUCTION

OREN LITWIN

W hat makes family magical?
Magic is the unexplained. It breaks the rules, it goes beyond the normal. Magic is uncanny. It is thrilling and terrifying. It is power and powerlessness, using and being used by vast forces far greater than we are.

Family can be like that too.

Giving birth to a child. Drawing strength from a parent, or fighting to break free. Watching your loved ones sicken and die, or cheering them on as they achieve great things.

This is the primal stuff from which our lives are woven.

This anthology asked authors for stories in which a family tie played a key role in the plot. And the selected authors—both award-winning veterans and talented newcomers—delivered, with works that were at turns poignant, tense, funny, and thrilling.

In "Bellwethers Know Best," Marion Deeds explores the trials of raising a powerful witch, especially for a family that once starred on reality-TV. In Joanna Michal Hoyt's "Legacy," a Mexican migrant laborer uses an ancient magic to protect his family. And a stressed-out young wife finds respite in a curiously slow-paced café, in W.O. Hemsath's "Coffee Break."

Misha Burnett contributes a story set in his award-winning

Dracoheim world: "She That Was So Proud and Wild," in which a young man who left his family farm and found love discovers that it is not so easy to escape the ancient ways of the country. In P.L. Sundeson's "Dead in First Grade," set in a post-catastrophe New Orleans, a young girl finds that life is not only for the living. And in a world besieged by magical terrorists, only one woman can find their weapons before tragedy strikes, in Elana Gomel's "The Dragon Detector."

Michelle F Goddard introduces us to "The Lake Cottage," a place of solace and bitterness, watched over by a mysterious guardian. Finally, in a kingdom devastated by plague, one man risks everything to obey his princess's command, in Frank Saverio's "To Find a Peach."

Each of these stories asks the question: what makes family magical? Each of them answers in a different way. Yet each of them is built on a fundamental truth: for good or ill, the greatest of magics that we have in this world is love.

～

This anthology was sponsored by thirty-five brave backers on Kickstarter, without whom this book's design would be nowhere near as beautiful as it is. The authors and I would like to thank our wonderful backers, including:

"How cool is this!", our Apprentice Mage;

"argleblick," Dagmar Baumann, J.F. Benedetto, Liz Owens, and "Keith West, Future Potentate of the Solar System," our Hard-Boiled Heroes;

J.J. Blacklocke, Tomas Bowers, B.E. Lewis, Olivia Montoya, Joshua Kristian Nielsen, Kay Pugh, Roberta Schoen, Kail Wright, and Deanna Young, our Codex Capturers;

Kat Hooper, Max Pearl, and Terry Weyna, our Tome Collectors;

Bill Capossere, Bryan Green, Ernesto Pavan, Eric S. Schaefer, "SwordFire," and Eron Wyngarde, our Digital Smorgasbord-Samplers;

Mark Carter, James Lucas, "Sydney," Heather Watson, Charity West, Andy K. H. Yeoh, our Fantasy-Lovers;

and several more who wished not to be named.

BELLWETHERS KNOW BEST

MARION DEEDS

Eulalie skipped down the hall, an amulet wrapped around her head to hold a cataract of lacy blue silk in place. Bracelets and tripled strands of beads ringed her arms. "Mom, I'm going out to play!"

Eden stood before the front door, one hand outstretched. "The Bracer of Erishkigal, please."

Eulalie rolled her eyes and slipped a red-and-black cuff off her wrist. As she held it out, a small book slid out from underneath the satiny stretch of lime green scarf she wore as a chiton and plopped onto the floor.

"And the grimoire," said Eden.

Eulalie handed it to her.

"And the Orb of Chios, while we're at it."

Pouting, Eulalie handed them over. "Grandma says she doesn't know how she raised such a killjoy," she said.

"Tell your grandmother that she's not helping."

Before Eden's mother made her unannounced visit, the ravens came. There were six. When Tom went outside one night to dump the compost they perched on the peak of the roof, staring down at him silently. They did not jostle, scold or fight; they sat still as sentries. And, like Eden's mother, they stayed.

"I don't know why she's here," Eden said. "Eulalie must have called her but she won't say why."

"Our daughter *is* a necromancer," Tom said, putting some dishes in the dishwasher. "And it's not like it's forever. It isn't. Is it?"

Women's voices, lilting and laughing, lifted Eden out of dream into wakefulness in their dark bedroom.

Tom groaned. "It's two-thirty."

"And a school night." She threw back the covers and went down the hall to the library.

The Bellwether-Hallgrove magical library held eight hundred

books, one hundred seventy-three scrolls, two hundred artifacts, both of Euphronia Bellwether's best-selling self-help books, the first volume of her incomplete memoir and *A Very Witchy Bellwether Christmas*. It had every single episode of *The Real Witches of Modesto, California* and *Bellwethers Know Best* recorded on crystal. Eulalie sat cross-legged on the floor, watching footage on the circle of farseeing-glass that hung from the reinforced ceiling by a silver chain. Flickering across its surface in a haze of pinkish light, Euphronia Bellwether and four fellow witches tried to complete a diversion spell during a driving rainstorm. It was the highest-rated episode of that show's eight-year run.

Even Eden paused, smiling, as an awning flapped and dumped a sheet of water over her mother's perfect blond curls. The episode played for laughs, but at the end, they diverted the flooding stream that was threatening a house whose bedridden resident hadn't been able to get out during the evacuation.

Eden shook herself mentally. "Pea-pod, you need to be in bed." She schooled her voice to calmness.

"I like to see Grandma," Eulalie said.

"I know, but you have to get up early." She stooped and put her hands on her daughter's shoulders. "You can watch her tomorrow, after you finish your homework."

"Grandma wants to talk to you about Aunt Emmaline."

"Not at two-thirty in the morning." Eden gestured and shut off the footage.

"No-ooo!"

"No whining. Back to bed."

"Can I take Grandma to the Plaza? She'd really like to go there."

"What? No." Eden recovered from her shock. "That's clear down in the center of town, filled with people. That's too overwhelming." Her daughter was gifted, but she was too young to know what the world of the veil was really like. Eden shivered every time she thought about her daughter entering that barren grayness.

Eulalie looked up at Eden, Tom's face in miniature, solemn. "I could do it. Grandma says I'm already a powerful neck—neckomancer."

Eden knelt down so her face was level with her daughter's. "You *are* powerful. And you don't have to live your life in service to a ghost."

Eulalie stared and didn't answer.

"Your grandmother doesn't have school in the morning," Eden said, "but you do. Off to bed, now."

"'Night," Eulalie said.

"I'll be in to tuck you in again, pea-pod."

She started for the door when the glass sparkled into pinkish life behind her. Euphronia flailed, slalomed down a freshet of muddy water on her backside and face-planted in a puddle. The highest rated episode. At least the woman could laugh at herself.

The image shifted to her mother's second show, the one Eden hadn't been in. In flowing script, the words *Bellwethers Know Best* filled the screen.

"Always the last word," Eden said. She pulled the door shut and locked it.

Muzzy from an interrupted sleep-cycle, Eden glared at the fifteen ravens perched along the edge of the roof as she left for work. "I'm not intimidated," she said. She walked past the lush herb border and got into her car.

On the way to work her phone pinged and Kaye's face appeared in the heads-up display. "We've got an intake to do at the third precinct," Kaye said. "I'm sending you the report. A guitar player at a pub summoned up a tide of the unsettled dead."

"Is everybody okay?"

"No injuries, no one's pressing charges, but he's pretty shaky and said he doesn't know what happened, so they bounced it to us."

"I'm on it."

Kaye narrowed her eyes. "You all right? You look a little frayed."

Frayed was exactly the word. "Interrupted night," she said.

"Your mother still?"

"Yeah, and Eulalie. Mother just won't leave her alone."

Kaye shook her head. "That's rough."

There wasn't much to the report. Jack Julian, age twenty-two, was playing guitar at a local brewpub when the place was flooded with shadows. People reported chills, overwhelming sadness, confusion and anxiety. "He'd just finished a Bach Sonata and was segueing into some blues when it happened," the intake officer said.

Jack Julian waited in an interview room. Eden studied him; slender, or maybe scrawny would be a better description, his head lowered, elbows on knees, his hands loosely clasped in front of him.

"I'm Eden Bellwether, from Magical Protective Services," she said.

He looked up. She saw The Look.

"Bellwether," he said. "You were on TV."

"A long time ago. Can I sit down?"

He gestured toward the other chair. "Is my guitar okay? I'll get it back, won't I?"

"Yes. It is a haunted object?"

He shook his head. "Just a guitar," he said.

"Was last night the first incident you've experienced?"

His eyes slid right and she watched the second of calculation while he considered lying. Then he sighed. "No. It was just the worst one. I've had a couple of smaller events in, I don't know, the past five or six months."

"When did you get the guitar?"

"I've had it for eight years."

"Any recent losses in your family, any trauma?"

He shook his head. "There's no family. I'm an orphan, my parents died when I was six. Why is this happening?"

"I'm not sure yet. Probably you come from a magical lineage and something triggered your gift. I'd guess it's necromancy but you'll want to get that tested. There are some amulets you can use to dampen the experience."

"Is that what you use?"

Eden shook her head. "No. I don't use anything. I'm an earth-witch. I grow things."

"But on the show—"

"Jack, let's stay focused on you. What do you know about the guitar?"

He straightened up and leaned forward in the chair. His eyes got brighter, more focused. "It's a Rosario Montoya. I found it in a pawnshop when I was just a kid; I couldn't believe it was just hanging there."

"Is Rosario Montoya someone important?"

"Well, yeah! Well, to guitar players. To some of us anyway." He launched into an explanation. Rosario Montoya was a luthier. She had made guitars in the 1950s and 70s. She made a guitar for practically every world-class rock star of that time.

"Did she die recently?"

"Uh, I think she must have died years ago. My guitar must be an early one," he said. "It doesn't have all the scrollwork and inlay like she did later, but the sound, the sound is like heaven."

Like heaven. Eden made a note on her phone. "I think you should get tested for necromancy. Do I have your contact information correct here?"

He looked embarrassed. "No. I'm squatting in the old Pritchard warehouse. I lost my apartment after the shadows came."

Eden had grown up with every privilege, and magic had still been a burden. Finding out in your twenties that you were magical because the remnants of dead people suddenly showed up whenever you played music—that wasn't an easy garden to tend. "I'm going to check in with you in a day or two," she said. "I may have some ideas, and I'd like to hear you play."

"I guess I have to stop playing in public," he said.

"We'll figure that out," she said.

From her phone, she copied her report to the PD and the office. Outside, on the wall of the precinct, a commercial for Mulekick Pizza played; a group of dancers, spinning pizza boxes in complete coordination, intercut three amateur dance mobs, one at the Plaza, one on campus, one in a crosswalk underneath the arch at 9th and I Streets. It was silly and fun; one of Emmaline's best.

A silver stretch SUV had pulled up behind her. Elegant scrolling graced the doors, all six of them. As she approached, the back passenger door whooshed down. Eden glanced inside. "Oh, no," she said.

"Good morning to you, too," Aida Sharp said. She held a container of popcorn. Aida based her appearance nearly one hundred percent on the looks of a certain type of female character from movies and episodic television of the late twentieth century. Her charcoal pencil skirt fit her like skin, black hair shone in a long bob. You could probably have sliced cheese on her cheekbones, and her lips were a shade of red not found in nature. "Let's talk." She carried a trio of popcorn blooms to her lips and munched them.

"I'm working."

"Oh, come on, Eden. Give me ten minutes."

Eden sighed. She might as well get this over with. She clambered into the seat facing Aida. The door whisked up and the autodrive car slipped away from the curb. Aida held out the paper container, a perfect replica of a cinema popcorn bag. "Imaginary popcorn? All of the taste, no calories and no kernels stuck in your teeth."

"No, thank you. What do you want?"

"We need your help," Aida said. "The studio is looking at projects. I've done some market testing, and I think it's time to bring back the show."

"Oh." Eden said. "Suddenly, *everything* is clear."

"I want to do *Real Witches of Modesto, California; The Next Generation*," Aida said. She touched a charm on her bracelet and the popcorn container vanished. "But your generation, except for you, is a bunch of talentless hacks, even Emmaline. And their mundane lives are boring too."

"Boring's nice," Eden said. "I like boring. I'd like to get back to it."

"Says the witch in law enforcement with the internationally famous pyromancer husband and a daughter who's already a necromancer."

"I'm not law enforcement, and Eulalie is ten. She's not going into your magical meat grinder."

"I wouldn't dream of asking," Aida said. "Honestly, Eden, do you think it was a picnic for us, your rebellious adolescence, your contempt for the shows? Emmaline *loved* the cameras, but you--"

"I think it was hundreds of hours of footage that were ratings gold," Eden said. "I'm sorry if that's not a picnic. Oh, wait. I'm *not* sorry."

Aida sighed. "What I'm trying to sell is your *mom*. Four no-talent witches aided by the spirit of a powerful one. And your mom, you know how well she does funny."

"So?"

"So, um, we need a necromancer to facilitate the meetings with the studio, and to help bring her through for the show."

"Studios have necromancers on staff, and artifacts."

"She won't come through for them. You know how your mom is about family. And we wondered if either you or Eulalie—"

"Are you kidding? As a necromancer, I barely move the needle. And if you come after Eulalie, I'll get a restraining order against you *and* Mother."

"Oh, I wish you *would*," Aida cooed. "Eden Bellwether goes into court to take out a restraining order against her famous dead mother. That would be some *delicious* footage."

Eden slapped the door release. The car jolted to a halt.

"Eden, wait. Let me at least take you back to –"

She got out and started walking back the way she had come.

"Eden! Can't we at least talk?" Aida shouted after her.

Back at the office she researched Jack Julian, whose parents had died in an accident fifteen years ago. His mother had magical gifts although the records weren't clear on exactly what. She'd been just like thousands of magicals probably, maybe using her gifts in small ways to make her family's life better. Jack had no criminal record and no documentation of a magical awakening. The luthier, Rosario Montoya, was more interesting...

It was twilight when she got home, carrying the Thai food she had picked up for dinner. Twenty-seven ravens lined the roof, staring at her. The house was quiet. "Eulalie? Tom?"

"Hey." Tom came out, took the bag, and kissed her. "How was work? More restful than home?"

"More productive, maybe. Where's Eulalie?"

"In the library. She finished her homework so I agreed she could watch that episode."

"I'll get her."

The library was empty.

"Eulalie?"

So was her bedroom, the bathroom and the den. Cold filled Eden and her heart hammered against her ribs. "Tom!"

He came out of the kitchen. "What?"

"Is she outside?"

"What? No." He wheeled and strode out into the backyard. "Eulalie? Eulalie!"

Eden rushed into the library and checked the artifacts. "Tom, the bracer's missing!"

She ran out into the front yard where Tom stood. Her husband clenched his fists.

"Damn it! I was on a conference call. Just a conference call!"

Eden said, "We need to think. Where would she go?"

The ravens rustled above their heads. Tom whirled and brought up his hand, sparks snapping from his fingers. Eden grabbed his arm. "Don't blame the ravens," she said. "This is *all* Mother."

"What is she *doing*?" Tom said, and he didn't mean Eulalie.

"The Plaza," Eden said. "Eulalie said she wanted to go there."

"Eulalie's walking all the way to the *Plaza*?"

It was a cool autumn night and the Plaza was not as crowded as if would have been in August, but there was a decent crowd eating cotton candy and sausage-on-a-stick. Where else would Euphronia Bellwether want to manifest? Eden tried to swallow her panic. They parked and followed the laughter and shrieks of amazement until they came to a circle of onlookers. Euphronia stood in the center, gleaming translucently, dispensing advice to a blushing, grinning tourist couple while scores of phones memorialized the moment.

"Where's Eulalie?" she said. Was her daughter in a trance in the middle of a crowd of complete strangers?

Tom scanned the crowd and pointed. "Over there. I'll go get her."

Their daughter stood at the edge of the crowd, flanked by tourists, her eyes gleaming. The Bracer of Erishkigal was clasped around her wrist.

"Eden! Eden, dear, is that you?" Euphronia called from the center. "It's Eden, everyone!"

Eden ground her teeth. She stepped away from the other onlookers and reached deep for her work voice. "Let Eulalie go, Mother. Right now."

Phones turned her way, and just that quickly, Eden knew that she had morphed back into her role from *Real Witches of Modesto, California.*

"We're just having fun!" Euphronia said, looking innocent and hurt. "She's nearly as powerful as my mother was, Eden! You must be proud."

"I can't believe how selfish you are," Eden said, and walked toward Eulalie. Tom knelt was kneeling in front of their daughter. Eden stopped with a little gasp. Her sister Emmaline stood behind Eulalie.

"Emmaline," Eden said. "How *dare* you rope my daughter into one of your stunts?"

"Look, everyone!" Euphronia beamed, looking around at the crowd. "The Bellwethers are all together again!"

Like sun-seeking flowers, every phone in the crowd turned toward them.

"She's fine. I'm right here looking after her," Emmaline said, putting her hands on her hips. She wore Euphronia's trademark pink, and her dyed blond curls looked stiff and damaged. Behind her defiant stare Eden thought she saw uncertainty.

Eden ignored her sister and squatted down. "Honey?"

Eulalie didn't answer. She stared past them at the glowing shape of the dead woman.

Eden shut her eyes for a moment. "Hold on to her," she said, and Tom took Eulalie's shoulders. Eden turned her daughter's tiny wrist free of the enameled bracer and, fighting a shudder, slipped it over her own wrist. The world receded as a cocoon of gray wrapped around her. She stood up.

The world of the veil felt wrong to Eden, it always had, flat and sere, barren. What if the artifacts trapped her here in this place where nothing grew, and she could never get back to her daughter, to her husband? She made herself breathe deeply and calmly, and turned to face her mother.

"Darling!" Euphronia said. Her delighted expression changed to one of hurt and shock when she saw the artifact. "Eden, can't we *talk*?"

Eden reached into the world of the veil and closed the link Eulalie had opened. Euphronia vanished. The crowd moaned with disappointment and a contingent started booing.

Eden, can't we talk? She couldn't believe her mother had used the show's catchphrase.

"Can't you just *talk* to her?" someone from the crowd shouted.

"Yeah, you are so *critical*!"

Pretending to ignore her sister and the angry, judgmental people around her, she turned back to her daughter.

"I want to talk to Grandma!" Eulalie shouted. "I was *helping*!" She burst into tears, a full-throttle meltdown. Tom picked her up, and they started for the car.

He stopped so abruptly that Eden bumped into him. "Oh, for God's sake," he said and Eden looked where he was looking.

"Hi, Tom," Aida said.

"Do not set her on fire," Eden murmured, "no matter how much we both want you to."

He shouldered past Aida and continued to the car. Eden heard the rapid tap of Aida's four-inch heels behind them. "Eden?"

Eden didn't turn to look.

"I guess you *can* move the needle," Aida said.

Eden spun around. "This was a *test*?" She raised her hands and Aida stepped back instinctively.

"Do not stick her in a thorn bush, no matter how much we both want you to," Tom said.

She turned away. Her head flared with pain. The crowd, cheated of a magical duel, increased its booing.

She drove home. Eulalie fell asleep before they pulled into the driveway. Eden carried her up to her room, dressed her in her Captain Marvel jammies, and tucked her in. "I'll stay in here with her," she said.

Tom kissed the top of her head and went down the hall.

Eulalie stirred and opened her eyes. "Don't be mad, Mom," she whispered.

"I'm not mad at *you*, pea-pod, but there will be consequences. We had no idea where you were."

"I was with Aunt Emmaline."

"Without asking."

Eulalie closed her eyes. "Grandma says Aunt Emmaline's divorcing Uncle Macon."

"Really?" That would be her sister's third divorce. "Go to sleep, Eulalie."

Eulalie slept and Eden sat in the chair. They called the type of show her mother had excelled at "reality," but it wasn't reality. With thousands of hours of footage, an editing suite and a certain gift, any producer could shape a narrative, or a character. How easily they had made elder child Emmaline the Supportive Daughter and Eden the Critical One. That's what she was now, shaped from the outside, but fully transformed; the critical one.

Tom pressed her shoulder. "I'll sit," he said.

She got up, but sat on the edge of Eulalie's bed. "I'm so stupid," she said. "Why didn't I see it?" She told him about Aida and the new show.

"Would your mother come back for that? I didn't think she was *that*... unfulfilled."

"I didn't either."

Euphronia was a witch by lineage and an entertainer by profession. She had always been clear-eyed about things. When Eden turned eighteen and didn't sign on for the seventh season, Euphronia had been on her side. It was Emmaline who had been angry. Eden knew now that her sister had intuited that without the conflict of the two sisters, the show would be less interesting.

When Eden brought Tom home for the first visit, during *Bellwethers Know Best*, Euphronia ordered the cameras turned off. And really, for all its silliness, *Real Witches of Modesto, California* had raised consciousness. A lot of the magical reforms they enjoyed now came directly from that show. Euphronia liked the spotlight but knew when to leave the stage. When Emmaline's attempt at a career in public relations was circling the drain and her second marriage had cratered, Euphronia had pulled the plug on *Bellwethers Know Best*, when she easily could have squeezed another season out of it. She wasn't just about attention. So... what, then?

"If they only need me to bring her through, I could do that, I guess. With the right tools."

"Can't Emmaline or one of the others open the link?"

"They aren't very talented. Apparently, Mother won't work with a necromancer who isn't part of the family."

"Well, what about linking her to an object? Like the bracer? That doesn't take as much juice."

"Yeah... Then we'd have a haunted object, and you *know* how well that works."

"You know Eulalie has to go on restriction," Tom said.

"I know." Eden lay down next to her daughter and put an arm over her. "I wish I could put my mother on restriction."

Even with all the redevelopment in town, there were still a few abandoned warehouses left, and it took Eden a while to find Jack's. A cluster of homeless people watched her as she walked up to the hanging door of the echoey space. As soon as she stepped inside she heard it, the sweet strains of Beethoven's *Moonlight Sonata*, the notes quivering around her. It was so beautiful it made her want to weep.

She walked across the empty main room toward the sound, and what she had taken to be shadows in the lightless building resolved themselves into a ring of the unsettled dead; only they *were* settled; they were as still and deep as a pool of water, drawn to the beauty of the playing and the piercing sweetness of the tone.

Jack sat on a rickety lawnchair, playing delicately. A sleeping bag lay against the wall. She waited until he brought the piece to a close and then cleared her throat.

"They're here," he said.

She nodded. "They're very calm. You are really good, and that instrument..."

"I know, right? It's beautiful."

"Heavenly," she said. "Jack, you want to go get a coffee?"

"We would have to do more research," Eden said, "but I think that isn't just an *early* Rosario Montoya guitar. I think it might be her first, her apprentice project, the thing that promoted her to journey level in her own mind."

"That explains why it's so simple," Jack said, "and so old. But what has that got to do with those drippy ghost things?"

"I'm going to oversimplify things for the sake of this conversation," Eden said. "Magic is a lot like science in one way; the better our tools get, the more we learn, and the more we discover that early theories were wrong. For centuries we believed that death was the end, and the essence moved on to a different plane or level. Then we decided that some people's essences remained behind because they had unfinished business, and they didn't 'cross over' or 'pierce the veil.'

"That's not exactly right either. Often remnants of the dead remain. They aren't harmful to humans, they don't necessarily have unfinished business. They just haven't fully made the transition. Humans are as connected to this planet as forests, whales or hummingbirds, and sometimes a piece of human energy remains with another person or with an object. We call those things haunted objects. I think that's what your guitar is. I think some of Rosario Montoya's energy went into it when she died."

"But why did it just start now?"

"Because she died six months ago. She was ninety-six."

"This would have happened with anyone playing my guitar then?" He brightened, then saddened. "So if I sold my guitar..."

Eden shook her head. "I don't think so. The tone of the guitar is beautiful, but your magical gift is probably part of this too. It's the combination of you and the instrument that is drawing the remnants we call the unsettled dead. And you aren't stirring them up, you're soothing them."

"So what does that mean? Audiences still don't like them. They get jumpy."

"We do get jumpy."

"Why do you say 'we?'" Jack said. "*You're* not afraid of the dead. You're a necromancer. I remember from the show. Your mother wanted you to work with spirits, and you'd be all 'I'll be in the garden!' and she'd yell—"

"'Eden, can't we talk?'" Eden said with a slight smile.

Tom had defrosted one of his famous lasagnas and he and Eulalie were making a salad when Eden got home. Over dinner she said, "Did Aunt Emmaline ask you to call Grandma?"

Eulalie looked down at the noodle she was cutting. "Will Aunt Emmaline get in trouble?"

"She's a grown-up, pea-pod. She can handle getting in trouble."

Eulalie nodded. "She said she needed to talk to Grandma." She put down her fork. "One time she said that you got everything and all she ever had was that crappy TV show. *She* said crappy."

"It's okay," Eden said.

When Eulalie had brushed her teeth, gotten into her jammies and Eden had read her a story, and Tom and Eden were in the family room, he said, "So *that's* what's going on."

"Mother was never fame-crazy, not really."

"Really?"

"Really, Tom, she wasn't. But if her daughter needed help..."

"Emmaline hijacked our daughter without even discussing it with us?"

"She probably thought I'd say 'no.'"

Tom sighed and propped one foot up on the other knee. "She *knew* you'd say no. She knows how you feel about necromancy."

"It's not the necromancy, it's the fake fame. It's—why are you looking at me that way?"

"Isn't it the necromancy a little bit?" he said gently.

"No. Eulalie's really gifted. I know that. I just want her to get to be a child."

Tom held up his hands. "Eden, you're an earth-witch, connected to life-energy, *and* a necromancer. Your abilities clash. But it's not like that for Eulalie."

"I'm over-protective?"

"When it comes to necromancy, maybe."

"Maybe." She sighed and stared at the carpet. "Emmaline really thinks she needs this new show. The thing is, she doesn't have much magical talent."

Tom snorted. "Much?"

"But she *is* talented. She's good at PR, she just picks bad clients. Those Mulekick ads are *good*! It's not her fault the pizza sucks."

"Would it be good for your sister to go back to having second-billing in an unscripted TV show with a ghost?"

"Whether it's good or not, it's what she wants. I put my wants ahead of hers last time."

"Eden. You were eighteen."

"Yeah, but..."

"Are you going to sacrifice *our* privacy for your sister? And your mother?"

"I don't *want* to," she said. "But right now I can't think of anything else to do."

She woke up and stared at the ceiling. After a while, she got up quietly, not wanting to wake Tom. She walked barefooted down the dark hall and went into the library. She sat down under the farseeing glass. "Mother," she said, "can we talk?"

"This place is weird, Mom," Eulalie said, holding Eden's hand as their echoing footsteps were swallowed by the warehouse. "Is Aunt Emmaline meeting us here?"

"I hope so, and bringing a friend of hers."

Aida caroled from behind them, "We're heeeere."

"In the big room," Eden said.

In deference to the rough terrain, Aida wore black trousers with a razor-sharp crease, a short black jacket with a peplum and shoes with only three-inch heels. Emmaline wore jeans and Euphronia's signature pink in the form of a fuzzy sweater.

The guitar music started, sweeping along the walls, something syncopated and bluesy, and Eulalie started jumping in rhythm. Even Emmaline tapped her hand against her thigh in time.

Aida said, "Is the music part of your grand plan?"

"A big part." Eden guided them in and introduced a nervous Jack to everyone. "Jack, will you play the *Moonlight Sonata* for Eulalie?"

"Uh, sure," he said, and started.

"Emmaline, I need to talk to you." She pulled her sister over into the corner. Through the walls, the unsettled dead seeped into the space, quiet and calm as the pure notes filled the room.

"I'll help you get what you want," she said.

"Don't do me any favors," said Emmaline.

"Oh, my *God*," Eden said. "Well, I *am* doing you a favor, even though you went behind my back and practically kidnapped my daughter." Behind Emmaline, Aida was watching them like a bird dog with the scent. Aida's drama-dar was legendary, and she probably wished she were capturing footage right now.

"Don't be so dramatic," Emmaline said. "She's my niece, I'm family. I'd *never* let anything happen to Eulalie."

"She *disappeared from our house*. I had *no idea* where she was." Eden swallowed as tears swelled her throat. "Do you have any idea what that's like?"

"Well, obviously not. I'm not like you, Eden. I don't have a great kid and a great job and a great –" Emmaline caught back a sob. "And a great husband. I have a half-assed job." She sobbed again and turned toward the wall. "I didn't even really ask, Eden, honest. I said I wished I could talk to Mom. And Eulalie said she'd call her and I just didn't tell her not to."

"Well, that sounds like Eulalie," Eden said. "She's got Mother's heart and Mother's supreme self-confidence. And ability. She doesn't even need the bracer, she just likes it."

"I know." Emmaline looked around and shivered. She couldn't see the dead but she sensed them. "So, what's the big plan? Did you just bring Aida and me here to lecture us?"

"I came here to pitch you a show." She walked over to where Jack was playing. Aida was scanning items on her phone, shivering slightly. Her shoulders hunched. Eulalie sat cross-legged at Jack's feet. Eden checked her purse. The bracer was in there if she needed it. She didn't think she would, though. "Eulalie?"

Her daughter looked up at her, smiling. "They like it. They like the sound. It makes them feel... happy."

"I know. Isn't it pretty? Aida, you okay?"

"Yeah. Sure. Fine."

"Okay. Do you think Jack's a good musician?"

"Obviously. He'd be a real draw if he didn't bring those... you know."

"Do you think with the right representation he'd appeal to a certain audience? People who aren't bothered by the unsettled dead?"

"Sure," said Aida, "but I don't see what that's got to do with us and an abandoned warehouse."

"Pea-pod, can you call your grandmother?"

"Uh-huh," Eulalie said. The warehouse filled up with pinkish light. Jack faltered for a second but kept playing.

"Oh, that's *lovely*," Euphronia said. "My, his connection to the entity in that instrument is strong, isn't it? Hello, dear. I'm Euphronia Bellwether."

"I'm Jack," he replied. "I, uh, wow." His fingers moved automatically, still striking the sweet notes. "I loved your show when I was a kid. Your shows, I mean. You were great. *Are* great."

"You're looking good, Euphronia," Aida said. Her eyes darted around the room, touching on Jack, Emmaline and Euphronia, and Eden could see the second when she made the connection. "Eden. That's *brilliant*."

"Not me. It was Mother's idea. We discussed it last night."

"Emmaline, picture this," Aida said. "A gifted musician whose playing attracts the dead, but also soothes the dead. His new manager is a Bellwether and her mentor is a powerful ghost witch."

"You mean Mom?" Emmaline said.

"There's never been a show like that, and it hits all the right notes. Hah! I meant to say that," Aida said. She walked away from the group, talking into her phone. Her voice shifted to chirpy mode. "Art? Aida. Forget *Real Witches*. I've got Bellwethers in a way you're going to love."

"Eulalie can't call Mother every episode, can she?" Emmaline said. "You'd never let her do that."

"No, I wouldn't," Eden said.

"But she won't have to, dear," Euphronia said. "Jack can summon me."

The musician looked stunned. Then he slowly nodded. "I'm some kind of necromancer. And the guitar helps."

Emmaline punched the air. "Yes! Bellwethers are back!"

"There's our title!" Euphronia said. "'*Bellwethers are Back!*'"

"*Don't Haunt Me, I'm Only the Guitar Player*," Jack said.

Eden beckoned to Eulalie and they left Jack, Euphronia and Emmaline talking, waving hands in the air, and laughing. Aida was discussing something about points with Art. And her daughter wasn't caught up in any of it. Eden felt herself smiling.

When they got to the door, Eden stopped. "Shoot," she said.

"What?"

"I forgot. Next time you talk to Grandma, please tell her to send those damn ravens home."

LEGACY

JOANNA MICHAL HOYT

May 20, 1954: California

David straightened up carefully. For a moment he let himself feel the pain in his spine and hips, the sweat sliding down his face and his back. Then he let those go and focused on Daniel, one row behind him, bent over the melon plants, his short-handled hoe moving quickly, rhythmically.

Daniel looked over as though he'd felt his father's glance like a touch; straightened a little too fast, winced, smiled. Not the quick eager way he'd smiled when David said he was old enough to come and work. This was steadier, a little rueful and more than a little proud. David smiled back and bent to work again before Gord the crew boss could come over and shout at either of them.

He would have liked to offer his son some easier way of being a man, work that wouldn't be hell on his joints, work that would let him marry a sweetheart and go home to her every night instead of leaving for months at a time. But that wasn't what he had to give. And maybe, after all, there was no easy way.

He straightened again when Martin, who was weeding the row ahead of him, gasped and swore. David looked over. He met, not Martin's eye, but the eye of the snake coiled a yard from Martin's foot which was slowly raising its head, opening its mouth, while its tail rattled in an accelerating rhythm. Martin was shaking all over, shaking in time to the rattling...

David's left hand reached into his pocket. *No*, he told himself firmly once he realized what he was doing. *No, you can only use that once, you'll need it more later. And if you get snakebite you can use it then, if you have to...* While his mind thought that, his body moved quick and sure, stepping forward, swinging the hoe up in a graceful arc as the snake turned toward him, bringing the hoe down in a sharp chop just behind the snake's head. Time stopped, swung slowly, began to tick normally around him again. Martin was still swearing, or praying, he couldn't tell which. Daniel was running down the row (taking care even in his haste, David noted approvingly, not to step on the plants), and kneeling next to his father, asking if he was all right, asking in a voice that made him sound younger than his sixteen years.

David put a hand on his son's shoulder. "It didn't bite me. It's dead, and I'm not. Everything's all right." He spoke in the slow level tones he'd use for a spooked horse, a screaming infant or a mean drunk.

Daniel bit his lip. Nodded. "Thank God," he said. Added, so softly that his father hardly heard him, "So that's part of it, too." Went back to work before Gord could swagger down the row to ask why they were slacking off.

"That's part of it too," David said. "But not for you, yet, not while I'm here." His hand brushed his left pocket again.

~

June 4, 1954: California

David squinted down at the paper. The candle made as much smoke as light, but work ate up all the daylight hours. It wasn't easy for Isabel either to take time to write in between taking care of her father and his mother and the little children, but at least she probably could find some daylight moments... He shook his head. He had no reason to resent her, and he wasn't really sure she had the easier part of the work. He thought about his mother's wandering mind and fits of temper. No, her part was no easier. Not that she wrote about the bad times; her last letter said "Your mother had a good day yesterday," and said nothing about the bad days before. But he knew how it had been last winter when he was home, and he doubted anything had gotten better.

"My dear Isabel," he wrote. "Thank you for writing. We are very well. Daniel works like a man, but he still laughs like a boy when Marcel plays his mandolin and we sing." Not mentioning that Marcel hadn't had time to do that since the time ten days ago when the thunderstorm drove everyone into shelter early in the afternoon. "I am glad Veronica is doing so well in school." In earlier years his trips North had paid for food and shelter for his family, but now that Daniel was earning too there was money for shoes and school fees for Veronica, and next year for little Jaime too. Veronica was clever—well, so was Daniel, but he was the oldest, there'd been no one to earn school money for him. "Give her and Jaimito a hug for me, and keep one for yourself. Daniel will write next time." Daniel was already asleep. "I know you take good care of everyone. Take care of yourself too. God bless you."

He stuffed the letter in along with the money, sealed the envelope, slipped out of the bunkhouse as quietly as he could—though most of the men were too tired to wake even if he'd stamped. He paused, passing Daniel's bunk. The boy's arms were curled around his stomach, his knees pulled up, his breathing jerky. David wondered what his son's nightmares were: he knew his own all too well, and they were mostly about his children. But Daniel was too old to tolerate being waked and comforted, and he'd likely resent being asked about his dreams in the morning. David went on out. The post-box, securely designed so that it was easy to put things in and impossible to get them out without a key, was a hundred yards from the bunkhouse. Tonight every one of those steps was going to take a separate, noticeable effort; he walked through fatigue as if through hip-deep water. Warm water: the night was windless, the hot air spread stifling along the ground. But the night was cloudless as well, the moon a thin crescent, the stars clear and thick and close as fireflies. He turned his face up to the light, let it wash through him. His father had said he'd once heard the stars singing. David paused to listen, was not troubled by the fact that he heard nothing.

But he did hear something, after all. Not celestial music, but a low angry voice in the dark, a voice that shook the way David's mother's hands did now, a voice trying to hold itself together against the shaking. He couldn't tell what it was saying.

"Maybe I will give it back," said another voice, also quiet, also vibrating faintly; but this one shook, he thought, with laughter not anger. "Maybe I will give it back, if you're nice to me." That was a man's voice. Gord's voice.

"That's my money." The angry voice was clearly a woman's, and as she got angrier she was forgetting to keep quiet. "It's for my sister and her kids. You have no right to that. You're a thief, that's what you are, a common thief, and if you don't give that back now I'll scream, and then I'll tell everyone..."

"And why will they think you were sneaking around in the dark with me?" Gord inquired, letting his voice match hers in volume. "I'll tell them a story or two about that..."

"No one will believe you." But her voice was lowered again; David wouldn't have caught the words if he hadn't been stalking toward them.

"No, Soli? Not if I tell them about the burn on your hip and the mole at the base of your spine and..."

"You've been spying through the crack in the outhouse, have you? I thought I heard a dog panting outside." Soledad—all of seventeen, and here in *el Norte* on her own—went on to describe Gord in picturesque and unflattering terms, but her voice was shaking harder, fear coming up thin and sharp under the anger.

"No one will believe you, Gord," David said low and clear. "Since I heard you, since I can tell them what you are. A thieving bully who spies on girls and tries to blackmail them."

"You think *el patron's* going to care?"

"No," David admitted. For one thing, Gord's English was good and David's wasn't, so *el patron* mostly just talked to Gord. For another... even if he understood, David didn't reckon *el patron* cared about Soledad. "But the rest of us will. And if you're hated by enough men... by the men who are all around you every working day... well, if you had an accident, how much do you think that would worry *el patron?* How hard would it be to replace you?"

"Harder than replacing you, if you had an accident."

"Here and now? Two to one." Soledad had control of her voice again, and she stepped in toward Gord and David, her head high, her hands out just below shoulder-level. David smiled. He hoped his Veronica would have that much grit—hoped that almost as much as he hoped she'd never need it.

"Any day. Any night. Go back to bed, Cruz. Stay out of this."

David had never liked being called by his last name only, but he had bigger things to worry about. He shook his head, then remembered Gord likely couldn't see the movement in the half-light.

"I'll go after you give her money back, I'm not too worried about any accidents you might arrange for me." That wasn't true, but he thought his voice sounded convincing.

"Or for your brat?"

David swallowed ice. Put a hand to his pocket. No, if something happened to Daniel he could deal with it. Fix it. Once.

"Give it back," David said. "Now." He took two steps forward, looked up into Gord's face (awkward, that—he was a good six inches shorter, and maybe fifty pounds lighter; not that that would stop him), put his hand out. Managed not to sigh with relief when Gord stuck the envelope into it. "Check the seal," he told Soledad, handing it over to her.

"Sealed. No slit. Thank you."

"I'm sure you can find a way to thank him nicely," Gord said in a particularly unpleasant voice, though he backed up as he said it.

Soledad took a step back from David too.

"I have a daughter, and a wife, and a mother, and a soul," David said. "Shall we post our letters together?"

June 30, 1954: California

Sunset, work over. David set his hands on his hips, pulled his spine straight, let his legs swing out long as they walked back toward the bunkhouse. On his right Daniel whistled "*A la puerto del cielo...*" On Daniel's other side Soledad whistled harmony. There was something to be said for being young, David thought. He was too tired to whistle, though he felt glad enough to appreciate the whistling beside him. Gord had spent most of the last month ignoring both David and Daniel, and Gord had been absent all day—no thanks to any accident of David's arranging, though David wasn't missing him. And tomorrow there'd be another two-week pay packet, and they were doing well, there'd be a little extra to send home—good thing, too, since Isabel wrote that Jaimito was sick again, and David knew medicine didn't come cheap—

Inside the bunkhouse he ignored the sweat-smell, concentrated on the smell of beans and tortillas, on the fact that he could finally sit down on something soft. He leaned back against the wall, felt his eyes closing...

He sat up sharply as the engines roared outside. Surely he hadn't been sleeping?

The bunkhouse door banged open. Headlight beams shone in

through it, backlighting the two men who stood there. Their faces were hidden by shadow, but their rifles were clearly silhouetted.

For a second everyone stood frozen; then everyone moved at once. Marcel crossed himself. Soledad sprang toward the window in the end of the bunkhouse, recoiled as another gun nosed across the sill. David stepped between Daniel and the gunmen at the door, glanced at the back windows and saw guns there too.

One of the gunmen said something in English, something David might have been able to understand if his blood hadn't been pounding in his ears. Even through that pounding he was able to make out the words of their translator's voice. Gord's voice.

"Stand still. Put your hands up."

He's arranged something worse than an accident for me, David thought wildly. *A kidnapping. I didn't know he was in with one of the gringo gangs, I've heard they're savage up here but I didn't think—Who have they come to kidnap? Me or Daniel? Or Soli?*

"Who do your thugs want?" David snapped, hoping he sounded more angry than terrified.

"Mind your manners," Gord said. "These aren't thugs, they're the Border Patrol. They want everyone."

More words in English. "Put your hands up, all of you. One at a time, tell us where we can find your IDs."

David bit his lip. He didn't have an alien card. So far as he knew, none of his fellow workers did, unless you counted Gord. David didn't have any connections in Mexico to move him to the top of the queue when they were hiring braceros, so when there wasn't work at home he came the desert way. Gord and *el patron* both knew perfectly well that they weren't hiring documented braceros—at any rate, they weren't paying the wages required for legal workers.

He put his hands up, thought of the bulge in his left pocket with something less than his usual assurance. Yes, that would get Daniel out of here, but where could the boy go? He wouldn't use it unless these men started shooting. He thought—he hoped—they weren't crazy enough to shoot.

Marcel was the first to say, in slow and careful English, "I got no papers."

"Come out. Move nice and slow. Keep your hands up."

Marcel did. Daniel and Soledad winced as he stepped through the door. No gunshot, no yelling, nothing to tell them what might be happening out there.

"What do they plan to do with us?" David asked in Spanish, pleased that his voice sounded reasonably steady.

Nobody answered.

David waited while three more men, and one woman, went out the door. None of the gunmen left to deal with them—there must be more of them stationed outside. David didn't see any good way of making a break. Seeing Daniel biting his lip, he stepped slowly past his son. "No papers," he said.

Six more men with guns and uniforms stood in the dirt yard by the bunkhouse. They were patting Martin down thoroughly, taking away his razor, his penknife. Motioning him along to one of a row of pickup trucks with wood-slat cages enclosing their beds. They looked like something farmers might take cattle to market in.

He eyed the nearest patches of shadow, looked back at the intent eyes of the gunmen. No, this was too big for him to fight. That was part of growing up that he'd hoped Daniel wouldn't have to learn for many years yet...

That was Daniel's voice behind him, saying "No papers," an octave higher than usual but fairly steadily. David held the same steadiness in his stance, in his eyes, as the man felt all over him. Took the knife. Took, also, the package from his left pocket; unwrapped it; squinted at the cross, the beads, the folded paper.

"I need that," David said firmly.

"For what?" the man asked.

"Shut up, Voss, we're supposed to let them keep church stuff," said another of the gunmen.

"Yeah, but what's written on it?"

"Who cares? We're not looking for master spies, Voss, we're rounding up wetbacks. Get on with it, we haven't got all night."

David understood that. He understood English reasonably well, when he wasn't panicking; speaking it was another matter.

Voss shrugged, stuffed cross and letter back into David's pocket.

"Where are you taking us?" That was Soledad, who had followed Daniel outside and was now watching unhappily as the BP man searched him. "What about our pay? *El patron* owes us two weeks." She spoke in Spanish. Gord didn't bother to translate until Voss asked him. Then he sighed, repeated her words in English, in a whining falsetto. Soledad spat at him. Gord stirred, stopped, catching the eye of the man who'd reproved Voss.

"We owe you nothing," Voss said. "You broke the law, you pay." David translated that, in an exaggeratedly brutish voice. Voss exhaled sharply, turned to search Soledad.

"Hands off!" she snapped.

"Leave her..." Daniel began. Stopped, as the man who'd reprimanded Voss pointed a gun in his direction.

"Keep your mouth shut and stand still," the man said to him, and to David, "Into the truck."

"Daniel," David said in rapid Spanish. "When you can help, even if there is danger for you, you help. When you can only make more danger for the one you want to help, you do nothing."

Daniel took in a shuddering breath. Said softly, as his father was marched away from him, "So that's part of it too."

"I'm sorry," David said, but he didn't think his son could hear him.

Daniel joined him a couple of minutes later. They were packed in too tight for David to give the boy any privacy even if he'd wanted to. He put a hand on Daniel's shoulder, felt how tight his muscles were.

"You will get out of this," David told him. "You will be all right."

"How?" Daniel demanded. David shook his head. This wasn't the time or the place to explain. "What about her?" Daniel added as Soli stepped onto the tailgate and clanged across to join them, her chin up, tears running down her face. David couldn't answer.

After that no one said anything for a very long time as the bunkhouse emptied and the trucks filled, as the trucks jolted down the road. Eventually Soledad said, very quietly, "Look at the stars."

~

July 2, 1954: Mexico

David, Daniel and Soledad stood together in the back corner of the caged truckbed, away from the worst of the sweat-smell but in the worst of the dust kicked up as the trucks jolted down the road. David had wrapped his shirt, and Daniel's, to keep the dust out of their mouths as well as keeping the blistering sun off their painfully tender scalps. Soledad had a bandana over her head, her lips pressed tight as she stared out into the gleaming dust, into the shimmer of heat. *La migra* had shaved all their heads to mark them in case they tried to slip back across the river and through the desert.

The road improved slightly as they pulled into the city. "Mexicali," David said. "If they leave us here it's not such a long way home... Soli, do you have money for bus fare?"

"I would," she said in a hoarse rusty voice, "if they gave me the pay they owed me."

"I have extra," he said, breaking off as the truck jerked to a stop. "It will be good to get out of here."

But ten minutes, later they weren't out of there. The men from the truck cabs had gone into a building—to make a report? To relieve themselves?—and were coming back, but the cages were still in place. "Excuse," David called to one in awkward English. "When can we go?"

"About an hour down the road," the guard answered without looking at David.

"What?" Soli shouted. "What city?"

The guard turned then, gave Soli a strange look. "Listen, it's not up to me," he said in a rather higher voice, and in passable though accented Spanish. "I'm just following orders."

"What do you mean? What city are they taking us to?" Soledad's voice had gotten lower, stronger. "We can't... in an hour..."

"Put you in a city and you'd come right back, they said," the guard said.

"What village, then?"

"Same problem, they said." The guard didn't meet Soledad's eyes.

Soledad opened her mouth but didn't seem able to speak.

"You're leaving us out in the desert?" David said, his voice rising with anger. "At this time of day? In this heat?"

"Look, man, it isn't up to me," the guard said. He wasn't gloating; his voice sounded as though he were the one anticipating being dumped in the desert.

David pressed up against the slats of the cage, stared at the guard.

"Better to be me, here, than to be you, there," he said. "You will dream about this woman for the rest of your life."

The guard kept his eyes down. "I don't make the policy," he said. "I just enforce it. I swore to uphold the law. Anyway I've got my family to think about."

"If you did not do this, they would leave your wife out in the desert? Your children?"

"Is he making trouble, Jacobsen?" asked another Anglo guard, in English.

"I'll sort him," Jacobsen said, waving the other man away. He set his face a foot from David's. Snarled, in very loud English, "You keep your trap shut if you know what's good for you." Fumbled with something at his belt. A sidearm?

No, a canteen, which he shoved between the cage slats at Soli before turning on his heel and stalking away.

"They're going to leave us without water?" she said.

"Not you, not quite," David said. Her hands closed on the canteen strap and she stared after Jacobsen, her back to David and Daniel.

David made a show of feeling the cage slats. "Shh, be quiet," he whispered to Daniel. "This one's loose. You can push it out a little way. You can get out."

"They'll shoot me! Anyway what about you?" Daniel whispered back. "And Soli?"

"They will not shoot you. We'll follow as quick as we can. Take this." David thrust the wrapped package from his left pocket into his son's hands. "Get out. Run. Hide. If Soli and I don't join you right away, stay hidden until you hear the trucks leave. Understand? If we haven't joined you, open this when the trucks are gone, and get back home. Your mother needs you. I'll come when I can."

"Give this to Soli," Daniel said. "Whatever it is. Get her out first."

"And let her risk getting shot?"

"You said..."

"No time! Do you trust me?"

"Yes! The way you stood up to that man..."

"Good. Go! *Andale!*"

David squeezed both his son's hand and the package. Said under his breath the four words his father had left to him along with the cross. Pushed the slat again—it had not been loose before, it would not be loose in another ten seconds, but it was loose now.

Daniel stared. Kissed his father on the cheek. Shoved the slat back, swung his legs over the tailgate, slid down, looking for a guard who did not come. Looked back to his father, who motioned him on furiously, made as though to climb down himself. Looked to Soli, who—as David knew and Daniel didn't—couldn't see him, any more than the guards could. Turned. Ran.

David gave one more push to the slat, which was firmly in place again.

"Leave that alone!" another returning guard said, glaring at him.

"Leave him alone!" Soli snapped. Turned. Stared.

"Where's Daniel?"

"He's gone," David said. Looked down. "I am sorry. I could only get one person out, and he..."

"And he is yours." She nodded. Then frowned. "But how...?"

"It is a long story."

"We have an hour for storytelling," she pointed out.

"You won't believe me."

"Make it an interesting lie and I'll forgive you."

He shrugged. Smiled a little. Looked to make sure Daniel was out of sight. Then told Soledad everything. About the cross his father gave him on the night when David's fever broke after everyone said he was going to die. The cross, and the note: *You can only use this once. For one person. To take away the thing that burdens them. Use it for yourself, it finishes with you. Use it for someone else, give it to them, they can use it once and pass it on again.*

He didn't get to talk to his father about it. His father caught the bus going North while David was still deeply asleep, really asleep at last after tossing in the fever for such a long time. His father didn't come back.

"Is that always how it works?" Soledad asked. "The one who gives it dies?"

"I don't think so, or how could you use it for yourself? I don't know. I hope not." He looked thoughtfully at her. "You believe me?"

"I'm afraid so."

"Afraid?"

She smiled a crooked little smile that looked as though it hurt her.

"After how you settled that rattlesnake—and that snake Gord—and then Daniel being gone—I guess I hoped you were magic, you could fix anything."

"I didn't use magic on Gord or the rattler." He thought a few minutes. "But I knew I could, if I had to."

"And now that's gone."

"That's gone."

The sun was straight overhead when the guards unbolted the cages and told their prisoners to leave. Most of David's people obeyed silently as he did, staring at their guards or at the blazing sand that stretched tawny and flat as far as they could see. Some cursed. Some prayed. Marcel grabbed the arm of one of the guards, said in furious Spanish, "You can't!" The guard pushed him down, walked away.

"At least he didn't shoot him," Martin said.

Soledad spat in the dust. Shook her head. "Waste of spit," she muttered. She stood with her face clenched like a fist as the trucks drove away, sending a last spray of dust against their faces.

"Which way do we go?' Martin asked eventually. "Anyone been out here before?"

"We're closer to Mexicali than to anything else, I think," Marcel said. "Better head back north."

"How long..."

"You don't want to think about it."

Their shadows were inching westward when Martin called, "Water!" It took a moment for David's mind to make sense of the words. His head was ringing with heat, his throat hurt, his shoulders hurt from little Jorge sitting on them, his feet hurt. He didn't know how much of the distance they had covered. He didn't want to know.

"Where?" he panted.

"There!" Martin took off running—how could he still run?--off to the right. David squinted after him, saw nothing.

"Mirage," he said, but couldn't make his voice loud enough to reach Martin.

"Mirage!" Soli shrilled. "Come back! The water's here."

Martin and Lupe ran on, knelt, and cupped their hands in water that wasn't there, recoiled from the heat that seared their hands and knees. They came back slack-faced.

"I can't go any further," Lupe said.

"There's water here," Soli said again, slipping the canteen out from under the burnoose she'd improvised. She took one swallow. Passed it to Lupe. "Pass it on," she said.

"There's not enough to do all of us any good," David objected. "Soli, keep it, he gave it to you..."

But Lupe had already taken a swallow and passed the canteen to Martin, who sipped and passed it to Marcel. It moved slowly, almost reverently, from hand to hand; David thought for a moment of the Mass. But there wasn't enough for even a mouthful apiece among so many...

"I have one too," Diego said, handing it to the man beside him.

When Soli's canteen came to Martin it was light, but not absolutely empty. He held it to his lips, passed it back to Soli without swallowing.

"Come on," he said.

He was walking down the road, he was walking forever while the heat burned away his eyes and his feet and his throat and his mind; and then the heat was worse all along his front, the heat and a kind of heaviness, and he tried to swing his feet forward but they wouldn't move. He realized after a moment that this was because he was lying facedown on the ground. It felt good not to move, despite the blistering heat on his face; but...but...

He had had the boy on his shoulders. He rolled to his side. "Jorge?"

"Martin took him half an hour ago," Soli said, bending over him. He knew her by her face; he wouldn't have known that rasp for her voice. "Get up, you have to get up!"

"No. Go. I'm staying here," he said thickly. "Daniel's safe."

"Is that what you want Daniel to do? Use whatever protection your family has for somebody else, and then once he doesn't have any magic just lie down and die?"

David opened his mouth to protest. Shut it. Sat up gingerly. Rose carefully, his body protesting with a fury that almost drowned out the heat. The sand was blowing over them again, glowing like falling stars, and he heard a faint thin music that slowly gathered strength as he made himself move his right foot forward, then his left. It might or might not have been the song his father heard once long ago.

He squinted through the painful haze of stardust to the city where his son was. "That's part of it too," he whispered.

Author's Note:

Operation Wetback really did happen in 1954. The Border Patrol rounded up close to one million undocumented immigrants from farms and factories across the country, shaved their heads and shipped them deep into Mexico. 88 people died after being left in the desert on a blistering hot day. Many more survived. Some families spent months or years trying to find out what had happened to their relatives.

COFFEE BREAK

W.O. HEMSATH

S *orry, I was inflating balloons.*

Despite it being the truth, Jess couldn't show up late to the second week of work and give Mr. Cardon that excuse. She'd heard stories of his intolerance. On a scale of one to "you're fired!" the truth was a solid eleven.

Jess licked her thumb and rubbed at some blue and pink paint flecks on her hand while maneuvering the car through morning traffic. Maybe the balloons and hand-painted banners were a touch excessive, but after two weeks on the rig, Troy was finally coming home tonight. Everything had to be perfect; she'd only get one shot to tell her new husband he was going be a dad for the first time.

Not that this was the perfect time to have a baby. After all, they'd been married a mere five weeks, and she was having a hard enough time juggling Mr. Cardon's ridiculous workload with this semester's impossible reading list. Of course, with how late she was running right now and the unfavorable traffic report on the radio, she might not have a job to worry about much longer.

Rows of red tail lights flooded the street ahead. The clock on the dash read 8:57, and she was still eight minutes away. She turned onto a side street, hoping for a shortcut. Up ahead, a colorful wooden sign with a croissant and steaming coffee mug caught her eye.

Sorry, I was getting you breakfast.

Now *that* was a decent excuse.

As she parked, the traffic report ended and that annoying new Crenessa song started. Jess gratefully killed the engine.

Nestled between a pharmacy on the corner and a small stationery store, the coffee shop had no windows or words anywhere, not even the name of the shop. It was simply a few feet of brick walls, a faded door, and the brightly painted picture sign.

The peculiarity of it gave her a sense of unease, but she shook the feeling off as she grabbed her purse, locked the car, and hurried down the sidewalk. There wasn't time to waste looking for anything else.

As she reached the café, a teenager on his bike came around the corner, riding on the sidewalk.

"Sidewalks are for pedestrians," she called. "Get in the bike lane."

He kept coming toward her with a challenge in his eye, and swerved around her, way too close to comfort.

She pivoted toward him in a huff, her hand protectively covering her abdomen. "You're going to hurt someone!"

The kid laughed and made a gesture behind him which her child would never be allowed to make. Jess's cheeks burned with righteous motherly indignation as she yelled after him again.

"And wear a helmet!"

More laughter, almost maniacal, erupted behind her. Two more teens on bikes raced around the corner of the pharmacy, heading straight for her. Forget reprimands; she barely had time to pull on the shop's door and duck inside before they reached her.

As the door shut behind her, the outside world fell unnaturally silent. Instead, a calming soundtrack imbued the air with sounds of wind chimes, rustling leaves, and a distant stream. The transformation of ambience was so startling, she couldn't help but sigh. Then the smells hit—warm tones of coffee, vanilla, and something that tasted like Christmas. She couldn't inhale deeply enough, but as she tried, all her anger and annoyance at the kids on bikes diffused and wafted away, as if carried on some unfelt breeze.

While not as bright as outside, the space was surprisingly well-lit for having no windows. It wasn't a harsh fluorescent light either, but a soothing, pleasant one that felt almost like early morning sunshine.

There was no one else in the shop, but a long padded bench dotted with pillows lined the wall clear to the back of the store. Jess followed the length of it past a few small bistro tables toward a display counter filled with danishes, donuts, and other carb-laden delights.

As she studied the pastries, a woman appeared from a back room wearing a badge with the name *Samaya*. She hesitated for a moment when she saw Jess, and then wiped her hands on her apron and gave a welcoming nod.

"Morning. What'll it be?"

Everything looked and sounded promising, but Jess had no idea what Cardon liked.

Cardon. Crap. How had she forgotten what a hurry she was in?

Why had she wasted time yelling at those teens and soaking in the ambiance?

Jess yanked her wallet out of her purse and scanned the display case again. The safest bet was to order a variety.

"I'm in a bit of a rush, so just give me three larges of your best blends and three pastries, whichever you recommend."

The barista nodded and started on the drinks.

"Actually, make it a half dozen pastries," Jess added, silently praying Cardon could be bought off with baked goods and caffeine.

Samaya opened the back of the display case and loaded up a paper sack. When she stepped over to the register and rang up the order, Jess's hand seized around her credit card. The total was staggering.

Samaya offered a sympathetic smile and gestured toward the bench. "You really should enjoy your meal here. The experience is half of what you're paying for."

Jess surveyed the modest interior again and cocked an eyebrow at her. No amount of relaxing soundtracks or pleasant smells was worth *that* much.

Samaya shrugged. "You can walk away if the price is too steep."

For a moment, Jess considered it. Troy would flip if he saw that amount on the credit card statement. But the price of showing up late to work, empty-handed, would be even steeper. Gritting her teeth, Jess thrust her card across the counter and gathered her purchases.

Samaya handed back her card with a receipt. "Come again soon."

Fat chance that would happen. Jess hurried for the door, hands filled with her purchases. She pushed the door open with her shoulder, squinting against the change in brightness.

Wham!

Something rammed into her, knocking her against the brick storefront and making her drop everything. Coffee scalded her stomach, and she grabbed her shirt to fan it away from her skin. A tangle of wheels, limbs and ruined pastries littered the cement in front of her.

The same two teens she had narrowly dodged before entering the shop scrambled to get back on their bikes. She probably should have checked to make sure they were okay, but her coffee! Her pastries! Her shirt!

"What do you think you're doing? You could've killed someone," she cried, stooping to pick up her fallen things. "Slow down and get off the sidewalk!"

Looking completely freaked by her outburst, and without so much as an apology, they mounted their bikes and peeled away, leaving her with a soggy bag and brown-stained shirt. Great. Now she'd show up to work late, empty-handed *and* un-presentable. At least when Cardon fired her, she'd have plenty of time to go home and change before picking Troy up from the airport.

No. Jess stood and faced the café. She was pregnant. She couldn't afford to lose this job and the health insurance it promised. Her benefits hadn't kicked in yet, but fifty-three more days and they would. She had to keep this job until then, whatever the cost.

She opened the door and stepped back inside, the inviting smells and sounds no longer able to wash away her frustration and urgency.

"Oh dear," Samaya said when she saw her. "Bathroom's over here if you want to clean up. I'll get started on some replacements."

"Yes, please." Jess tossed the ruined goods into a trashcan by the door and rushed to the rear corner Samaya had gestured to.

After a couple minutes of cold water and what felt like forever under the electric hand-dryer, Jess emerged from the bathroom with her blouse hopefully presentable enough not to grab Cardon's critical eye. Either way, she had to leave. At this point, she'd be almost a half hour late for work.

Samaya, bless her heart, stood outside the bathroom with a new tray of coffees and bag of pastries ready to go.

"On the house."

The tightness in Jess's chest loosened a little as she took the replacements. She didn't have the time or money to argue. "Thank you," she said, forcing herself to slow down long enough for it to seem sincere before she bolted for the door. When she reached it, she nudged it with her shoulder, checked for impending collisions, and then hurried to her car.

After securing the drinks, she turned the keys and that stupid

Crenessa song started playing again. She changed the station and noticed the time on the dash said it was only 9:03.

Perfect. On top of everything else, now her car was breaking too.

Jess entered the office building with one hand clutching the pastry bag and her briefcase, the other carrying the coffees in front of her like a shield.

Cardon emerged from his office scowling, and she cringed. Exactly how late was she? She stole a quick glance at the clock on the back wall, and her heart jumped.

Only 9:13? That had to be wrong.

Cardon zeroed in on her. "Where are yesterday's reports?"

"Right here, sir, ready to go. And I'm sorry I'm late. I was getting coffee. Take your pick." Jess handed him the tray and fumbled a stack of folders out of her briefcase while he read over the descriptions Samaya had jotted on each cup. Selecting one, he took a sip, and his eyes widened in surprise. He lowered the cup, eyed it briefly, then drew another long sip.

"Terrific brew."

The panic gripping her started to release. Cardon wasn't smiling, but he wasn't scowling anymore either. He passed back the two remaining coffees and grabbed the files from her while ogling the pastry bag. "Any bear claws?"

Jess checked the bag and beamed. Samaya had included not one, but two of Cardon's favorite.

"They're both yours," she said, offering him the bag.

He tucked the files under his arm and pulled out the pastries with a satisfied grin. "You're a good addition to the team," he said, lifting his cup toward her in a toast before taking another sip and heading back to his office. "But don't be late again," he called over his shoulder. "Today's reports are on your desk."

"Of course, sir. I promise I won't—"

His door closed before she could finish, and the rest of her panic dissipated. She wasn't fired.

When she reached her cubicle, however, her relief vanished An impossibly large stack of papers towered next to her keyboard. They'd take all day at the office and all night at home to finish. She sank into her chair, pulled a muffin from the bag, and started in on the first report, trying hard not to think about how the drive home from the airport might be all the time she'd get to spend with Troy that night.

After a few reports, she glanced at the clock on her desk, and an uncomfortable feeling settled over her. She compared her desk clock to the one on the back office wall, the one she had assumed was wrong when she arrived. Both clocks matched.

But how? There was no way it was only 9:13 when she got to work. Given the time she left her house, the time spent in the coffee shop, and the time stuck in traffic, it should have been closer to 9:30. Could both clocks at work be broken? Maybe it was the one at home that was off.

She returned to her work, trying to be satisfied with that explanation, but no. The time in her car had matched her house clock when she left. And it matched the office clocks when she arrived. They couldn't *all* be off by the same amount of time, could they?

And what about the bike collision? Those kids were in the exact spot they had been in when she entered the shop. Could they really have gone around the whole block in the time she took to order and pay? And why would they be riding laps like that?

All day, there was an incessant scratching at the back of her mind, a stray thought begging to be let in, to be considered.

It was almost as if while she had been in the coffee shop, time had—

No. How could she even consider something so crazy? Was this what pregnancy hormones did to a person? Jess tried to bury herself in her reports.

But what about the song? Sure, top forty stations repeated hit songs on their playlists, but twice in fifteen minutes?

By lunch, she couldn't take it. It was the stupidest idea she'd ever had, but if she didn't prove to her silly pregnant brain that the coffee shop did not actually freeze time, she would never be able to focus enough to finish her reports. Disproving the theory would be easy; all she needed was something to throw. She filled her empty cup with water and drove with it back to the shop.

Once parked, she made sure there was no one on the street to witness her experiment and lifted the cup of water from the console. She approached the shop, opened the door, and slipped halfway in. Before she could talk herself out of it, she heaved the cup as high over the sidewalk as she could and slammed the door as fast as possible.

"What are you doing?"

Jess froze, hand on the closed door, and turned to see Samaya staring her down from the back counter.

"I... um..."

Jess searched for words to fill the silence. She couldn't bring herself to admit out loud that she thought she'd found a magic coffee shop where time stood still.

Samaya studied her for a moment, then her stern glare dropped as if it had been a mask. A smile danced behind her eyes.

"I was right. You're the new one, aren't you?"

Her current demeanor made Jess even more uncomfortable than her critical stare from moments before. The new one? What was she talking about?

"I wondered when it would pick someone else," Samaya continued. "Thought it might be you this morning, but I never know until they come back a few times. Takes most people a few visits, but you, you're quick." She laughed at Jess's bewildered face and nodded toward the door. "Well, go on. Check."

Jess's rational mind fought against the electrifying thrill of possibility that danced in the air. The way Samaya was smiling—it couldn't be, could it?

Holding her breath, she pushed on the door. The moment it cracked open, her cup and water fell, splashing at her feet.

Everything around her seemed to shift. It was impossible. It had to be impossible.

"You look like you could use a drink," Samaya's voice called from behind her. Jess turned around. Samaya was carrying two steaming mugs to one of the bistro tables. She sat down, took a drink, and patted the empty bench beside her. "Like I said before, it's best enjoyed here."

～

Sixty days working at Cardon's had felt like forever, especially with her frequent coffee shop visits, but her benefits had finally kicked in and not a moment too soon. Not knowing her due date, thanks to irregular cycles, was killing her. It had to be late April or early May, seeing as Troy left for the rig three weeks after the wedding, but her new OB had agreed to an ultrasound anyway to pinpoint a more specific date.

The lights in the ultrasound room were too dim to read while she waited for the technician to begin, but Jess didn't worry anymore about reading and working in every spare moment. Closing her eyes, she gave herself permission to savor the here and now and relaxed into the padding of the reclined exam table. The disposable liner crinkled under her like tissue in a gift bag, and a faint trace of coconut hung in the air—probably the technician's lotion or something. Between the steady humming of the machines and the warm air from the vent chasing away the late October chill, the room was calm and comfortable, perfect for finally seeing her baby.

The technician's typing stopped, and the sound of her chair rolling closer on the tiled floor prompted Jess to open her eyes.

With one hand holding a bottle of gel, the technician gestured toward Jess's overstuffed bag in the corner. A textbook and file folders poked out the top.

"School or work?"

"Both," Jess said, lifting her shirt and rolling down her waistband. "Online master's and a desk job."

"Both full time?"

Jess nodded. She also wrote novels part-time, had finished three scrapbooks, and recently learned to crochet, but it didn't seem polite to brag.

The technician swirled a massive glob of clear gel onto the rounded edge of the ultrasound wand. "Where do you find time for it all?"

Jess suppressed a smirk. "I drink a lot of decaf."

"Are you sleeping enough?"

"Definitely." Eight hours every night at home, not to mention what felt like another eight hours between projects on a surprisingly comfortable café bench. She was well-rested, and for the first time in forever, she felt on top of everything. Her increased productivity had even impressed Cardon so much, rumors of a promotion floated around the office.

The one downside was she couldn't share it with Troy. That was one of the few things Samaya had explained—the shop chose one person at a time, and she was the current one. If another person was in the shop, the magic wouldn't work. It wouldn't have been such a problem, except the other rule Samaya had explained was now that Jess understood the magic and accepted it, she had to come make a purchase every day or the café would choose someone else. This meant a lot of expensive coffees, fights with Troy about credit card statements, and trying to come up with believable lies since the truth was both crazy and impossible to prove.

She hated keeping things from him, but if this one secret meant she could do, feel, and be better than she had ever been before, it was worth it. Besides, as soon as he saw the ultrasound photos of their baby, all the suspicion and tension mounting between them would melt away. Who could be upset about coffee when they were staring at their new child?

She braced herself for the cold touch of the gel, but it felt warm as the technician pressed the wand into her abdomen. The pressure against her full bladder made her wince for a moment, but the screen in front of her soon stole her focus. Different black and gray shapes morphed in and out of view as the technician slid the wand around.

Then there it was—a perfect little body with perfect kicking feet. Jess fought back tears. There would never be a moment better than this one.

The baby's legs spread apart as the technician held the wand steady with a surprised laugh. "Well, there she is." The legs kicked again. "Looks like you might have a little dancer on your hands."

Jess's breath caught in her throat. "She?"

The technician froze. "Oh my goodness. I was supposed to ask if you wanted to know the gender. I can't believe I blurted it out. That's not like me. I am so sorry."

A daughter. They were having a daughter! Jess tried to memorize every amazing detail of the little body wriggling on the screen before her. The technician still looked panicked, waiting for a response.

"It's fine," Jess reassured her. "We were planning to find out gender. I just didn't think we'd be finding it out so soon."

The technician, visibly relieved, resumed moving the wand. She clicked on the screen to record a measurement.

"Looks like it's not soon at all. You're measuring twenty weeks and two days."

The room felt suddenly cold. Jess must have heard wrong.

"I can't be more than fourteen weeks." She stared at the technician for confirmation, but the technician chuckled.

"Oh, you're definitely further along than that."

"I can't be. Measure again." There was an edge to Jess's voice now which filled the room with palpable tension.

"It's not an exact science," the technician offered. "The date could be off by a few days."

"It's off by six weeks. We didn't get married until August 1st."

"If you're worried people will think you got married because you were preg—"

"You don't get it." Jess's voice projected louder than she intended; it bounced off the walls of the tiny lab, but she didn't care. She needed to make this woman understand. "My husband is religious. He insisted we wait." She locked eyes with the technician. "We did."

Silence hung in the room, long and cold and awkward. The paper under Jess rustled as she waited for the technician to believe her, to acknowledge the error. The technician cleared her throat, avoiding eye contact as she resumed measuring and typing.

"I think maybe we should just finish the ultrasound. Who you share the results with—or not—will be up to you."

Jess's hands trembled as she drove to the coffee shop. She needed to make her daily purchase and come up with a plan. In her peripheral, the incriminating envelope of black and white pictures taunted her from the passenger seat.

It was ludicrous. Troy was the father. There was no way she was twenty weeks pregnant. But what could she say? That the ultrasound machine malfunctioned, and the tech was incompetent, and it only *seemed* like she cheated on him before their wedding?

She had to hide the photos and tell him a different due date. A week or two he might chalk up to error. But six weeks? Six weeks might as well be forever. It was almost as long as she'd been working for Cardon. Almost as long since she discovered the coffee shop.

A cold idea bit the edges of her mind, and her chest tightened.

The coffee shop.

If she estimated ten hours working on projects and eight hours sleeping on the bench, seven days a week, for eight weeks—

Her knuckles whitened as she clung to the steering wheel. It added up to six full weeks.

A few broken speed limits, a crooked parking job, and some thunderous steps later, Jess barged into the patron-less cafe. Samaya stood at the back, drying a mug.

"You lied!" Jess stomped back to the counter. "I wasn't getting extra time."

Samaya raised a challenging eyebrow but continued drying. "There's no such thing as extra time. I never said there was."

"But all this time I've been in here working—day after day, week after week—you let me think time was standing still."

"It is." Samaya jutted her chin toward the door. "Outside."

How could she stand there, drying that stupid mug, not realizing what a huge problem she'd created? Jess slapped the counter with her palm. Samaya didn't flinch.

"You never told me I was still aging. That *my baby* was still aging. You never told me I was stealing from our future."

"You're right." Samaya set the mug down and whipped the dish towel over her shoulder. An uncharacteristic hardness fell over her features. "I simply said you can walk away if the price is too steep, and that if you do, it'll choose someone else."

Jess took a step back as realization set in. Samaya would not be giving her any kind of apology or solution; she was giving her an ultimatum.

Keep using the coffee shop or walk away forever.

Jess turned to the familiar bench stretching out before her, empty and inviting. Every moment she stayed would cost her future and possibly her marriage, if she hadn't lost it already. But without the shop, she'd never finish her degree or novel, let alone keep up with work and sleep. Cardon would never give her that promotion once her productivity dropped. Troy would be upset when she failed classes they couldn't afford for her to retake. This shop had made all her dreams possible. How could she walk away from the most miraculous thing she'd ever had?

Samaya's voice, cold and curt, pierced her thoughts. "Are you going to order or not?"

As Jess agonized over the impossibility of her choice and the injustice of it all, her stomach fluttered. She tried to will the anxiety away and fought back hot tears, refusing to cry in front of Samaya.

Her stomach fluttered again.

And again.

Serenity washed over her as she realized the flutters weren't anxiety. They were her daughter—moving, stretching, growing. Jess marveled at the sensation. It felt... magical.

Resting a hand on her stomach where her daughter had kicked, Jess drew in a deep breath and met Samaya's expectant stare. In that moment, she knew there really wasn't a choice at all.

Without another word, Jess turned and exited the shop. From that moment on, the only magic that mattered was the one growing inside her.

SHE THAT WAS SO PROUD AND WILD

MISHA BURNETT

A t the old fuel station off the highway Jenni went in to get some snacks for the road.

Marc stayed with the truck and had the attendant fill the two jerry cans he kept in the back as well as the truck's tank.

"Headed up country?" the attendant asked, using an expression Marc hadn't heard in years.

Marc nodded. "I've got folk in Carne Shant."

"Not as bad as it used to be," the attendant observed. "There's stations up in the delves now."

"I'd rather be prepared," Marc said. "Better to spend wisdom than earn it."

The attendant grinned at that. "Old church?" he asked.

Marc shook his head. "Not anymore."

Jenni came back with warm fudge wrapped in waxed paper and bottles of ginger soda.

Marc paid the attendant as Jenni climbed in, then waved as he drove off.

"Friendly people," Jenni said.

"They can be," Marc observed.

"Funny thing..." Jenni began, giving Marc a sidelong glance, "There was a sign at the register about not taking coins unless they're rolled. The last place we stopped had the same sign. What's that all about?"

"Old church," Marc said absently. "They don't use paper money."

Now Jenni's look grew sharper. "What do you mean?"

"I mean they don't use paper money," Marc said irritably, focused on the road. It was hard packed dirt and not really built for motorized traffic. Things might be better than they used to be, but that wasn't saying much. Change came hard to the delves. "They pay for everything with coin. If they weren't rolled everybody would spend all day just counting money."

"Hmmm," Jenni said. She tried a bite of fudge, washed it down with soda. "This is good. Want some?"

"Not right now," Marc said.

Jenni looked out the window. Now that they had left the highway, everything was green. On either side of the road were fields of... hay, maybe? Big boxy cattle stood here and there, chewing. It was like a page from a picture book. *The Girl Guides Visit a Farm.*

She was from the city, and she and Marc worked at the same supermarket. He was a produce manager, she was a bookkeeper. They'd started dating and it had gotten serious—serious enough to plan this trip together for her to meet his family.

It had seemed romantic back in the city, but here in the hinterlands she was feeling more and more uncomfortable. Marc was a great guy, with an old-fashioned charm. He opened doors for her and brought her flowers. He treated her like a lady, which was something that she would have claimed she didn't want before she met him.

The delves, though... This was like something out of the last century. Marc carefully passed a horse-drawn carriage and the driver —an old man wrapped in layers of shawls—glared at the truck darkly.

"How far is your folk's farm?" Jenni asked.

"Maybe ten mile from here," Marc said. "Be there ere darkfall."

He was even starting to talk like a country boy again. When she'd first met him she'd found his accent cute. Over the last few years he'd started talking like everyone else, losing the odd little habits of speech. Now they were coming back.

Take the boy out of the country, she thought, but you can't take the country out of the boy.

Beside her Marc scanned the fields on either side of the poor road, watching for memories. Five years ago he'd left the farm by this road, on foot, with all he owned in a rucksack. He'd caught the bus to the city a dozen yards from the station where he'd just filled the truck.

He hadn't planned on ever returning—no, he *had* planned on *never* returning. It was supposed to be a clean break from the old land, the old homestead.

The old church.

Then he got the letter from his father and he knew he had to go back, one last time. Some business must be conducted in person.

They passed more wagons and a few people on foot, but no other motorized vehicles. Everyone stared at the truck as it went by, as if they'd never seen such a thing before.

Marc half-expected he would miss the turn to Carne Shant, but he found himself signaling for a right turn automatically when he saw the stone pillar beside the road, long before he could read the weathered words on the side.

Home again, he thought bitterly. *Blessed be.*

There was a fuel pump in front of the feed store, with prices chalked on a sign beside it and a faded banner in the window of the diner that read, "Diner's Club Accepted." Aside from that it looked just the same as when he had left. A handful of buildings, scrubbed brick and whitewashed wood, staring at each other across a dirt street. Butcher. Hardware. Yard & Dry Goods. Cypherer.

"Cypherer?" Jenni wondered.

"What folks up here call a magus," Marc explained.

Then the round-domed bulk of the church and once past that they were headed back out of town, just like that.

Jenni was peering around as if looking for the rest of the town.

"That was it," Marc said, grinning despite his dark mood. "You just saw all of Carne Shant."

"It's... cozy," Jenni decided on.

"It's a dump," Marc said. "You can say it."

"Marc," Jenni's voice was pained. "It's your home. It's part of you. I came up because I wanted to see where you grew up. I came up here to meet your family."

Carefully Marc reached over to touch Jenni's shoulder. "Thank you. But we won't be here long. It's not my home anymore. My home is back there, with you."

Ahead the fields were more obviously cultivated and Jenni could recognize the crops. Corn, beans, and wheat. She had enough experience with bulk pricing to know that these were prosperous farms.

The drive that Marc pulled into ran arrow-straight between rows of brilliant green corn. The house at the end of the drive was freshly painted yellow with blue trim, the barn behind it—three times as big as the house—just as freshly painted in firehouse red. Beside the house was a neat plot of vegetables, and behind that a delightfully colored flower garden. Big wooden boxes stood in the middle of the flower garden and after a moment Jenni realized that they were bee hives.

"You never said your folks were rich," Jenni said softly as Marc pulled in to park beside the drive.

He gave her a puzzled glance, then looked back to the farm. "They're just middling busy," he said. "Not what a body'd call rich."

A man came out the door of the house and crossed the porch, his arms wide in welcome. His hair was neatly cropped silver, his shoulders broad and his stride strong. Marc's father, Jenni thought. Looks just like him.

Marc got out of his truck and the then walked around to open Jenni's door and help her out.

His father stopped so quickly that he looked as he was about to topple over, shock on his face.

Jenni looked quickly down at herself. *What,* she thought, *is my skirt too short? Should I be wearing a scarf over my hair? What didn't you tell me, Marc?*

Marc's father recovered and gave a weak smile. "Miss," he said with a nod. "I'm Amos Grenn."

"Jenni Dvarich," she replied, smiling weakly back.

Mr. Grenn called back to the house without taking his eyes off Jenni. "Seph, why don't you come out here. Marc has a friend avisitin'."

The woman who came bustling out of the house didn't seem old enough to be Marc's mother. She was tall and tanned, her hair blond and fine as corn silk, tied back with a twist of fabric.

"Hello, Marc," she called cheerfully, then turned her attention to Jenni. "Welcome, stranger," she said, her face and voice full of genuine warmth.

"Miss Dvarich," Mr. Genn said, only stumbling a bit over her name, "This is my wife Persephone. Why don't you head on inside for a bit. Seph, maybe the young lady would appreciate a glass of tea while me and the boy attend to his conveyance."

Jenni had time to shoot Marc a dark glance—*what have you gotten me into?*—before Mrs. Grenn enfolded her in a warm blanket of chatter. "You come all the way from the city? Such a long way—I've never been there, of course, but we hear tell of it. At least you had a nice day for a drive. I hope the roads weren't too crowded. Marc didn't tell us he was bringing a guest, but make no never mind, you're welcome. I've got sweet tea cooling right now—or maybe you'd prefer lemonade? My home is your home, dear girl, come on in and make yourself comfortable..."

Mr. Grenn waited until he heard the screen door close behind the women before he spoke to his son in a harsh whisper. "What under Heaven were you thinking, bringing that person here?"

Marc sighed. "Nice to see you, too, dad."

"Do not take that tone with me, young man!"

"You know what?" Marc turned back to his truck. "This was a mistake. Let me just fetch Jenni and go."

"Bringing that person to homestead sure enough was a mistake, but—"

"That person has a name!" Marc roared at his father. "Her name is Jenni and I love her. I am going to marry that woman. I thought maybe I could try one last time to get through to you, but I can see that's not going to happen."

Mr. Grenn stared at his son for a long moment, sadly shaking his head. "Boy..." he said at last. "You know that's impossible."

"Getting through to you is impossible? Yeah, I know that. I've always known that," Marc seemed on the verge of tears. "I just thought... never mind, it's not important."

"Marrying that girl is what's impossible," Mr. Grenn said softly, kindly. "She looks like a fine young woman and I can tell you're taken with her. But your bride is in the fields. She's out there now, waiting for you. You know that."

From inside the house Jenni could feel the stormclouds of tension gathering above Marc and his father, but Mrs. Grenn—"Oh, call me Seph, honey, everyone does"—seemed unconcerned. She led Jenni through a formal dining room and into a kitchen that took up nearly half the ground floor. There she fussed over the girl, making sure her chair was comfortable and plying her with pecan pie and cold tea sweetened with honey.

"Now tell me all about yourself," Seph said with a smile. "Your people are from the city, are they not?"

"Yes, I grew up in Leeshore, that's in the southeast, on the water. My father's a fisherman," Jenni found herself responding automatically. Then, a bit hesitantly, "I get the feeling that Marc's father wasn't happy to see me."

"Amos isn't overfond of surprises," Seph said. "That's no reflection on you."

Jenni nodded, unconvinced.

Seph got to her feet. "Now I'd best get the stove lit and fixings started if we're going to eat before midnight."

Jenni stood. "I'll help."

Seph waved her back to her seat. "You'll do no such thing, young lady. You just sit yourself and we can talk while I fix. It's nothing but chicken pie I'm making."

"I get the feeling that Marc left, well," Jenni tried to be diplomatic, "under rather strained circumstances."

"Oh, true enough," Seph agreed, getting flour and measuring bowls from a cupboard. "Hard words were spoke—half of them from a man who should have been grown enough to think twice."

"Why?" Jenni asked. "What was the fight about?"

Seph opened an icebox—Jenni noticing with some amusement that it was really stocked with blocks of ice, was not a refrigerator—to get eggs and a cruet of cream. "Not my story to tell, dear. But don't you fret about it. They are good men, both of them. Love will win out. It always does, you know."

"I brought Jenni up here because I thought if you maybe saw her, got to talk to her, you'd understand," Marc said, struggling to keep his voice under control.

"I do understand, boy," Amos replied in the same tight tone. "I understand that you want to run away from your duty, and you're pouting like a baby because you can't."

"*It's not my duty!*" Marc took a deep breath, then went on. "This is my life, and the homestead is not part of it. Not anymore."

"It's in your blood, boy. This ground is part of you. You can't change that. You got roots, son, roots that go back hundreds of years."

"I'm not the one in the family who grew out of the ground."

Amos' hand came up so fast that Marc never saw it, just felt the pain from the open-handed slap across his face.

"*You do not talk about your mother that way,*" Amos hissed.

"It's true!" Marc protested. "Isn't that was this is all about? My bride? Out there in the fields? What *you* want for me? Well, I don't want it, and I'm not doing it. I have a woman, a real woman. A human being, not a... pumpkin."

"You will show some respect or so help me the next time I lift my hand it won't be empty." Amos' voice was cold. As cold as death.

"I love my mother," Marc said, pleading. "You know that. You know that I have nothing but respect for her. But that is not what I want for my life. I can't live here. I need my freedom. It's why I had to go before, and it's why I will have to go now. Without quickening a bride."

Amos turned away from his son to look back up at the house, then out at the field of corn behind the house. At long last he spoke, "Son, it's not that simple."

"Yes it is," Marc countered. "It is exactly that simple. I won't do it, and you can't make me."

Amos turned back. He glanced at Marc, then looked down at his muddy work boots. "You don't get it, do you, son? You lived in that house for sixteen years. You don't think you left any hair behind?"

"When I first saw you I thought maybe you were Mr. Grenn's second wife," Jenni said. "You don't look old enough to be Marc's mother."

"Oh, bless you girl," Seph smiled at her from across the table. The chicken pie was in the oven and the kitchen was full of the wonderful smell. "It's the summer, of course. I always look my best in the summer. I assure, though, Marc is my very own baby boy. Amos, too, to be honest."

Jenni giggled at that.

Seph sighed. "You never stop raising boys, you know. You just get them half-civilized enough to turn over to their wives to finish the job. If we ever do."

The front door opened and Seph raised her voice, "Now, I know those aren't boots I hear on my front hall."

Amos' irritated voice came back, "I've got to sit down to take 'em off, now, don't I, woman?"

Seph looked back to Jenni. "You see what I mean? It never ends."

Jenni grinned. She'd come to like this woman, so different from anyone she'd ever met before. Jenni's own mother was a hard woman who raised six children and kept the house for a man who was on the sea for weeks at a time, chasing the schools of pollock and bluefish. She'd grown up with love, but precious little laughter.

When Amos and Marc came into the kitchen, unshod and freshly scrubbed from the pump house, they wore identical grim expressions. It was uncanny how similar father and son were; they seemed to be two pictures of the same man, taken twenty years apart.

Seph rose to fill the uncomfortable silence with the clatter of plates and glasses, getting everyone seated properly around the table and then bringing out the chicken pie in its iron pot to set in the middle of the table.

Amos nodded his silent approval and then reached to either side, taking his wife and son's hands in his own. Jenni followed suit uncertainly, holding Marc's hand with her right and Seph's with her left, completing the circle.

Amos bowed his head and spoke softly, "We have so much before us and for this we are thankful. We have so many blessings, and for this we are thankful. There are others not so fortunate, and by this we are humbled. We shall make an offering in their name to They who watch over us, that those in need are someday as blessed as we are this day."

The family then said together, "Blessed be." and Jenni managed to echo them just a half-beat off.

Then there were plates to pass and glasses to fill and the mutter of "please" and "thank you" around the table for a time.

"I've turned down the linens in Marc's room," Seph announced. "I'll set up the guest bedroom for Jenni after dinner."

"Thank you," Jenni said. Then, "I'm sorry we didn't give you more notice I was coming."

"No trouble at all," Seph replied. "The unexpected guest is Heaven's ambassador." She turned to her husband. "Maybe you want to butcher me up a hog for tomorrow?"

"We won't be staying," Marc said quickly.

Amos nodded. "Marc and me have business out in the green tonight. He and the young lady can be on their way in the morning."

Seph gave the two men a sharp look, then turned back to Jenni. "I've a pair of gum boots you can wear."

For a moment there was silence. Then Amos said, "Seph, that ain't needed."

"Of course it is," Seph said easily. "That back patch is powerful muddy, and it'd be a shame to spoil those pretty shoes."

"Mother, I don't think—" Marc started nervously.

"Not thinking is exactly what the pair of you is doing," Seph said sharply.

"Persephone," Amos said in a warning tone. "The boy and I have this handled."

Seph looked past her husband to her son. "Marcus Aurelius Grenn, do you or do you not intend to marry this woman?"

Marc swallowed hard. "I do," he said. Then in a small voice. "If she'll have me."

"Then you need to tell her," Seph's voice was firm. "Or else send her on her way and apologize for wasting her time."

"Tell me what?" Jenni asked.

"This ain't her business," Amos protested, but weakly.

"*Somebody* tell me what is going on here," Jenni said.

With a deliberate poise Seph picked up her fork and returned to eating.

Jenni looked from father to son.

Amos shot Marc a glance tight-lipped with anger.

Marc flinched away from his father's glare, then sighed and started talking, looking down at his plate. "Our family has certain... traditions."

He looked across to Seph. "Mother, may I explain?"

"I'll keep no secrets from Jenni," Seph said. "I've nothing to be ashamed of."

"My mother is a hamadryad," Marc said quickly, then looked up to Jenni.

Jenni looked at Seph, who smiled and nodded, then returned to eating.

Jenni looked back to Marc. "And you were going to tell me this... *when?*"

"I wasn't going to," Marc admitted. Then, with a glare at his father, "Because I had left the homestead. Left the old church."

"You can't deny who you are," Amos began, and Seph waved him to silence.

"But if you're half dryad—" Jenni began.

"I'm not," Marc said angrily. "I'm all *him.*"

Jenni looked from father to son again.

Seph spoke. "Dear, Marc *is* Amos. Just as Amos is his father Enoch before him. And Enoch was Michael."

"How?" Jenni asked.

Marc looked down at the table, blushing. "Dryads don't add any of themselves to their children. They just... carry on the male principle."

Jenni's eyes grew wide. "When you said that Amos was your little boy...?"

Seph laughed. "Oh, no, not literally. That would be dreadful, wouldn't it? I was quickened to be Amos' bride. His mother is rooted now, out in the forest. You can visit her, but she's not likely to talk to you. She never did care for strangers."

Amos raised an eyebrow. "Your little boy, am I?"

"Hush, darling, not now," Seph said. "Go on, Marc, tell her the rest."

"When my father wrote me he said that it was time to quicken my bride," Marc said. "I brought you so that he'd see that I wasn't going to. I already have the woman I want."

Jenni reached to touch Marc's hand. "Thank you. And... I guess I can see why you didn't tell me all this before. But it's okay. Really, I can accept this." She turned to Seph. "A hamadryad, Well, I've never met one before, but I like you, no matter what you are."

"There's still a problem, though," Marc said grimly. "My father didn't wait. He began the quickening without me."

"And that means...?" Jenni asked.

"She's already begun to live," Seph said. "She's made for Marc. Just as I was made for Amos. She needs to be with him, to be his bride. She can't be anything else."

"I have to kill her," Marc said. "Before she awakens. That's the kindest thing to do."

Amos ran the blade of the ax over the whetstone. Without looking at his son he said, "Do you want me to say I'm wrong?"

No reply.

"All right, then. I was wrong." Amos looked up.

Marc held out his hand. "That doesn't matter now. Let's just fix this."

Amos held on to the ax. "It does matter, son. I interfered in your life. I just figured you needed a nudge to get your life in order. I didn't know about Jenni."

"Well, you do now," Marc put his hand on the ax and Amos released it. "I suppose they'll be scandalized at the meeting hall."

"Oh, forget the meeting hall," Amos said. "None of them would dare to breathe a bad word about my boy. I just want you to be happy."

"I wish mother hadn't told Jenni."

Amos frowned. "She's always got a good reason for everything she does," he said slowly.

"I know. I just wish I knew what it was."

"Secrets are like splinters, girl," Seph said, digging through her closet. "If a body don't get them out, they fester."

"It just, well, it's going to take some getting used to," Jenni admitted.

"Of course it will, honey." Seph came up with a pair of bright red rubber boots. "Here we go. I knew I had them somewheres. Amos got these for me years ago, and they're tight on me. They should work fine for you."

"Thank you." Then, in a small voice. "Is it really necessary?"

Seph sighed. "It is, dear. Justice would be for Amos to do the deed himself, since he did the quickening. But he conjured her for Marc, and it's best for the man she's made for to put her down."

"It seems so cruel."

"Cruel would be to let her live without hope," Seph said firmly. "Amos is my man and I was made for him. I know I may not always talk about him gently, but gentle's got nothing to do with love. Love is doing what needs doing, no matter if it hurts. Sometimes love means causing hurt, if it needs doing and there's no one else who cares enough to do it."

Seph sighed. "Amos is a fool half the time and damned fool the other half, but he's mine. My life is that man, and without him I would just wither up and die, like a tree when you cut the taproot. That body in the ground isn't anything alive, and it can't be without love. It'd just be walking dead, and that's no way to be."

Jenni nodded slowly. "Yeah, I guess I understand."

"Do you love my son?"

"Yes."

"Then your place is to stand beside him and give him the strength to do what has to be done." Steph wrapped her cloak around her. "Moon's up, girl. We'd best get the menfolk moving."

The moon was a few days short of full and the night was clear. The four of them didn't talk as they crossed the yard to the patch of ground behind the barn.

There was nothing left to say.

She's not a person yet, Marc told himself. *She sleeps in the earth. She won't even know it's happening. It's better this way. Kinder.*

The ax handle was slick with sweat. He wiped his hands on his dungarees, one at a time. It helped a little. *Let me strike true. Let me make it quick.*

The little patch was surrounded by a knee high fence. Nothing more than a symbolic barrier. He stepped over it easily. Vines crisscrossed the damp earth, spotted with bright flowers, white, yellow, blue. Tiny gourds hung from the vines, glossy and green, ripening towards yellow, spotted in places with the orange they would blossom into at the end of the year.

Marc stepped carefully through the vines. Heard the others stop at the fence.

In the center of the patch was her.

She lay on her side, curled around herself. Naked, except for the mud that slicked her. Her hair a golden cascade down her back, shining in the moonlight even through the mattes of soil. In all respects a young woman, attached to the rooted plants by a thick stem that emerged from her stomach. Where her belly button would be if she were human.

She isn't human. She isn't breathing. The church teaches that she doesn't have a soul, not yet, not until she draws her first breath.

Marc raised the ax.

This isn't murder.

"*No.*"

A figure was hurrying through the vines to fall to her knees beside the still form of the hamadryad.

"No, you can't," Jenni said. "You can't. Not for me. I won't let you."

Jenni cradled the body in her arms, looking up at Marc, pleading. "She deserves to live."

Marc lowered the ax. He could feel his shoulders trembling from the strain.

"Jenni," he said softly, "you know I didn't want this."

"But you have it," Jenni said. Gently she cleared dirt from the unmoving face. "I love you, but I won't let you kill for me."

"She's not alive," Marc protested.

"She could be," Jenni said. The face beneath her fingers was smooth and lovely. "Look at her."

Then the figure moved in Jenni's hands. Her eyes opened, and her lips parted and she drew in a breath.

Jenni stroked the side of the hamadryad's face. "It's okay," she said. "It's okay. I'm Jenni, and I've got you. What's your name?"

"Sibyl," Seph said from the fence. "Her name is Sibyl."

"Sibyl," Jenni repeated. "That's a pretty name."

The stem connecting her body to the ground cracked and fell away, withering in moments.

Sibyl looked around frantically, then her eyes found Marc behind Jenni's shoulder and she smiled.

Marc went to his knees, dropping the ax. Marc and Jenni held the new creature between them.

Seph watched the three of them, a smile on her lips.

Amos looked at his wife, then at his son, his son's woman, and the dryad that clung to them both.

"Guess I best butcher that hog after all," he muttered.

DEAD IN FIRST GRADE

P.L. SUNDESON

A s an only child who did not play with many other children, Emma Peters had no one to tell her what school was or should be like. She was sure, though, that your teacher was not supposed to be dead.

❧

Emma knew the days of the week, and she knew Thursday was a Work Day. So she was startled to see Daddy, in his dark gray suit and tie as always, waiting outside their gate that cool September morning. She threw herself down the steps and hugged him around his waist. "Daddy! I'm glad you came. Mommy said you had work."

Daddy stroked her head. "I couldn't let my little girl go to her first day of school without me."

"I'm glad." She couldn't recall ever seeing him smile at her or Mommy. Maybe because he and Mommy were *seprated*, a word she'd heard Mommy use, and he was sad about that? He didn't live with them — she couldn't recall when he ever had — though he came for dinner twice a week.

"Why not a Monday, Daddy?" she asked as her parents walked her toward the school. She was excited, but a scary little spot buzzed in her chest too, and so she talked to help herself ignore it.

Daddy and Mommy glanced at each other. After a moment Daddy cleared his throat. "Everything's on reduced hours because of the labor shortages, hon. Since the Big Plague, there just aren't enough... people... to do all the jobs."

Emma knew about the Big Plague, though it had all been over with before she was born. "Lots and lots of people died?"

"That's right," Mommy said. "That's why your school starts later and ends earlier. Your father and I, we've had to make... adjustments... like everyone else."

She knelt, so that her eyes were on a level with Emma's, and turned Emma to face her. When she got down on your level and looked at you with The Serious Face, you knew it was Important. And that too was scary.

"It's a big day for you today," Mommy said. "And we want you to have fun. But... you may see some strange things today. Maybe even frightening. They won't hurt you, though, and you can tell us about them later. Okay?"

Emma nodded.

Daddy cleared his throat again. "C'mon, hon. We'll be late."

Emma's school was a big reddish-brown building with lots of windows. A grassy yard flanked it on the Royal Street side; a long black iron fence separated the yard from the sidewalk. Older boys and girls raced around the yard, some squealing as they played on the red and yellow plastic slides and the climbing bars. Emma wondered if she would get to play with the boys and girls.

Daddy and Mommy led Emma through the double doors. In an office, a lady with a sign on her desk — Emma read it: SECRETARY — smiled at them. "Mr. and Mrs. Peters? Good, good. I'll see Emma to her class. Remember, you'll need to pick her up at two."

"Two o'clock sharp." Mommy knelt and hugged Emma. "You be good now, hear?" She waved from the doorway, and then she and Daddy were gone. For a terrifying instant Emma wanted to run after them. She wished she had her favorite doll, Mrs. Renfro, to hold and talk to. *No,* she thought. *You're a big girl now.*

The secretary lady led her by the hand down a polished wood hall to a long windowed room full of desks. Children about Emma's size, a sea of strange faces, stared at her as the secretary lady seated her at one of the small desks. It was hollow inside. The top had once been smooth wood, but letters ("TR," "JEK") and signs she didn't know were carved into it now.

The secretary lady consulted a list and called out some names. Three boys and four girls came up to the green chalkboard at the front of the room, and the secretary led them out. Later Emma would realize they were last year's first-graders, being taken to their second-grade class. Now, though, she was annoyed. They were already getting to go out and play?

Another lady came in as they left. She strode with a *click-click* of heels up to the chalkboard, took a piece of chalk, and wrote in a spiky handwriting:

MRS. OMINOR

She set down the chalk, turned, and looked around at them. "Good morning, children. That's my name on the board, Mrs.

Ominor. One of the things you'll learn with me is how to read and write your names. And other things, of course."

Emma stared, fascinated. Mrs. Ominor was about as tall as Mommy. Her age Emma had no idea of; an adult was an adult; but their teacher was clearly not *old* old. She stood straight, wearing a dusty blue jacket and skirt, with a little lacy white thing peeping out at her pale throat. Her face was pale too, almost as white, with dabs of red on her lips. And her sleek straight hair was the blackest hair Emma had ever seen: like the glossy black feathers on the crows and ravens that hopped after bits of bread in the park. Emma did not have the word "dramatic" yet, but if she had she would have seized on it and pointed to Mrs. Ominor.

There was something strange about her face, though. Emma didn't know yet what it was.

Mrs. Ominor picked up a green notebook from the desk in the corner and began to do something she said was "calling roll." Emma didn't know what that meant, but she got the idea quickly. When her name was called, she said in a clear voice, "Here."

As she waited for roll call to finish, she glanced around the big room. Atop the chalkboard ran a strip of paper with the alphabet, each big letter then the small, like a mommy with her child. A big piece of paper on a stand depicted a wheel with different colors, RED and YELLOW and GREEN. Cutouts of cheery rabbits and ducks dressed like people romped around the walls. A basket of crayons and drawing paper lay in sunlight under one window.

"All right," Mrs. Ominor was saying. She pointed to the clock above the door. "How many of us know how to tell time?"

A bunch of hands went up, and Mrs. Ominor began to talk about the little hand and the big hand. Emma wiggled in her seat and swung her legs. Was this all school was going to be, talking about stuff she already knew?

In the back corner stood two stacks of books, one stack short, the other tall. Emma wondered what kind of stories were in them. She slid out of her chair and started toward the stacks.

"And where do you think you're going, miss?" Mrs. Ominor's voice was pleasant, but it was hard too. Emma froze. All the kids had turned to stare at her, and her face felt hot.

"Just... to look at the books," she said in a tiny voice.

"Did anyone give you permission to leave your desk?"

Emma shook her head. She hated to break rules (well, actually, she hated to be *caught* breaking a rule). She gulped back tears.

"No? Well, we have rules in school, Little People." Mrs. Ominor's voice was level. "If you want to speak, you hold up your hand until I call on you. If you wish to leave your seat to visit the Little Boys' Room or the Little Girls' Room —" The children tittered. "— Hold up your hand. Young ladies and gentlemen do not leave their desks at will."

Her gaze came back to Emma, and suddenly the little girl realized what was so strange about the woman's face.

When Mommy talked, her face *moved*. She frowned or smiled, or squinched up her eyes or opened them real wide. Mrs. Ominor's face did none of those things. Even as she spoke it remained blank, as though, Emma thought, her face had *forgotten* how to move.

"All right, Miss Peters, you may sit down."

Face aflame, Emma crept back to her seat.

The morning crawled by. At last a bell rang. "Recess," Mrs. Ominor explained. "Run out and play. The rear yard only, please. Come back to your seats when the bell rings again."

The rear yard was not the one Emma had seen earlier. This was bigger, surrounded by brick walls, with grass and dirt and a big tree at one end with a patch of mud under it. At the other end, several girls were chalking squares and numbers for hopscotch on a stretch of concrete.

"Boy, the old bat really came down hard on you, huh?" said a blonde girl, Beverly something. She smiled at Emma.

Beverly was a fraction shorter than Emma, and the tanned arms and legs left bare by her dark blouse and skirt looked strong. Her chin was small and her nose pointed. If Emma had been a few years older, she would have been wary of the way Beverly's smile flashed so often and yet somehow never reached her narrow dark eyes. But Emma was six; and so she smiled uncertainly back.

"I don't like her," said another girl. "She's mean. And weird."

"I know," Emma said. "Her face doesn't even move when she talks. What's wrong with her?"

"You don't know?" Beverly looked surprised. "It's 'cause she's a deader."

"Dead-er?"

"Silly." Beverly giggled. "That's when the dead come back to life. Wanna play hopscotch with us?"

"Mommy?" Emma asked. "What's a deader?"

It was after dinner, and she and Mommy had settled onto the couch with their latest storybook. The TV was only on for a few hours each day, and mostly showed grownup programs, so Mommy had taken to reading to her. Tonight they were deep into *Space Cat Goes to Mars*.

Mommy set down the book. "Where'd you hear that word?"

"The girls at school."

Mommy sighed. "I might've known." She set *Space Cat* aside. "I guess you're old enough.... What do you know about the Big Plague?"

"The meezles —" Emma had only heard the word, so she imagined it was spelled like that "— moo-tated and killed lots of people, because the doctors didn't have the right shots."

"Mutated," Mommy corrected. "That's right. People were getting sick and dying all over the world, including here in America."

Emma felt a sudden stab of fear. "Could I get it and die?"

"No," Mommy said firmly. "Because the meezles are gone. A very smart group of doctors and scientists made it disappear. The doctors and scientists used... forces they didn't completely understand. They were desperate, and decided they had no choice. A long time ago, people might have called it 'black magic.' It worked and saved us... but it changed the fabric of the world."

"How?"

"In a lot of ways. Food tastes different from when I was a girl, and colors look different, and the engines in cars don't run like they used to. Summers here used to be very long, but now winter starts sooner, and we get snow and even blizzards.

"The big change, though, is that — people can be called back from the dead."

Emma shivered. "Like Miss Goldy?" Miss Goldy had been her hamster. Emma had found her lying stiff and cold in her cage a month ago. She and Mommy had held a funeral and buried her in the backyard.

"Sort of. It won't work for animals, though, only people. And only people who've been... gone for a very short time. Their memories fade pretty fast.

"Companies found that their labor shortage, their lack of workers, could be solved by using the recently dead. After all, they're legally dead, so they don't have to be paid the same as 'breathers' — that's what the dead call us. They don't have the same legal rights we do. It's a lot cheaper to use dead workers."

"Don't the deaders complain?" Emma found the topic scary, but she didn't want the conversation to end.

Mommy shrugged. She was not smiling any more. Despite the lamplight, her face looked... dark, somehow, as if shadows lay on it. "They seem happy enough. This way they get to use their skills and knowledge." Mommy laughed, but it sounded funny. "Better than..." She stopped.

"And Mrs. Ominor is one of 'em?"

"Her face is blank when she talks? Then that's it. I knew the school district had hired some, but it's hard to tell, they walk and talk just like we do. Except the lack of expression. And—" She stopped again. Then: "Never mind. Honey, you know there's nothing to be afraid of, don't you? They won't hurt you. It's just like having a live teacher. Understand?"

Emma nodded. But she still wondered.

"They don't feel pain like we do," Beverly announced. "You could drop a lit match on a deader's foot, and she won't even feel it."

It was early October, and Beverly and Emma were scuffing through the fallen leaves under the tree in the schoolyard for the sheer joy of hearing them crackle and crunch. "Autumn," Mrs. Ominor had told them. "The trees are preparing for winter."

Since the first day of school Emma and Beverly had become

inseparable. Beverly's last name was Sanders, so she sat right behind Emma, and they would whisper and pass notes. This incurred Mrs. Ominor's wrath. Twice already she had made them both stay an achingly long hour after school for talking in class.

True, there were things about her new friend that Emma did not care for. Beverly had an irritating habit of pinching Emma's arm, hard, when the latter was not looking, saying innocently, "Just trying to get your attention." When Emma made a mistake at hopscotch, Beverly would laugh with the other girls, which annoyed Emma. She thought a friend shouldn't do that.

One day they had been walking home with Beverly's mother, a stout woman with a dreamy expression who always let the girls range ahead of her. Suddenly Beverly darted to the curb. "Look!" A small blue bird was flapping its wings — Emma saw that one was injured — and struggling to take off.

"Take that," Beverly said with glee, and smashed the little body flat with one black shoe.

Emma gasped. "Why'd you do that? It was hurt!"

Beverly shrugged. Already it seemed her mind was on something else. "It wouldn't have lived anyway. A cat would have got it. Wanta see if Ma will buy us some ice cream?"

The memory of the little crushed bird body on the concrete bothered Emma for a long time. But she had never had a friend her own age before. She had the notion you were supposed to be loyal to your friend, no matter what....

Now she said, "I don't believe it. Why wouldn't burning hurt 'em?"

"Dunno. That's what my Aunt Lucy says. She says when we're asleep, they come creeping into our rooms and suck out our tears! And they hate us and wish we were like them."

Emma shivered.

Beverly's dark eyes gleamed. "We could stick a pin in ol' Ominor, and she wouldn't even squeal."

"You'll get in real trouble, Bev."

Beverly scowled. "I don't care. I hate her and all the deaders. I've got a surprise for her if she makes me stay after school again." She kicked harder at the leaves. "C'mon, slowpoke, keep up!"

The blow fell late that morning during Matching. Mrs. Ominor would hold up a card with a colored shape on it, and then call on someone to name an item with the same color. Emma liked the game, but Beverly paid no attention. She was drawing with several crayons. Suddenly she tapped Emma's arm. "Look."

Emma took the paper. On it was a stick figure drawing of Mrs. Ominor; you knew it was her because of the long black hair and red lips. A knife stuck up from her head, with big blue drops spurting out. Despite herself, Emma giggled.

"Blue drops instead of red," Beverly whispered. "She doesn't have blood like—"

"Just a moment," Mrs. Ominor said coldly. "I see some young ladies are disrupting the class." She set down the spelling book and marched between the desks to stand over a quivering Emma. "Let me have that, please." For an instant Emma smelled something from her... a whiff like meat that had sat out too long in a warm kitchen. Then it was gone.

"It's just—" Emma began.

"I don't care. Give it to me." She snapped the paper from Emma's hand and stared at the drawing — without expression, of course. "I see. What's your explanation of this, Miss Peters?"

"Nothing..."

"You think sticking a knife in someone is funny?"

"No," Emma whispered. She wanted to shrink to mouse size and scurry out of the room.

Mrs. Omninor swiveled her stare to Beverly. "And I see Miss Sanders is trying to look as if butter would not melt in her mouth. Very well. Detention for both of you this afternoon, and tomorrow you can both explain to the class about the origin of that phrase." She crumpled the drawing and stalked back up to her desk. "Now, before we were so rudely interrupted, we were on Blue. Mr. Sikes?"

At 2:00 the final bell rang, and the class packed up their school bags and fled. All except Emma and Beverly, who stayed, long-faced, in their seats.

Mrs. Ominor regarded them from her desk. "Quiet, please, children. You may work on your homework for tomorrow." She drew a thick book from her briefcase and opened it.

"Damn deader," Beverly muttered. It was a soft sound, Emma could barely hear it, but Mrs. Ominor glanced up. "This is detention, not recess. No talking."

Mrs. Ominor was the only first-grade teacher who gave homework: usually to look at the pictures in their reader and try to puzzle out the words beneath. Emma had already whizzed through the whole book, despite Mrs. Ominor's instruction not to, and was bored with Jack, Jill, Sally, and Spot. She spied a *Highlights* magazine on the corner table. She wished she had grabbed it before the bell rang.

Time ticked by, oh so slowly. 2:11. 2:12. Cars hissed by in the street below.

At 2:14 Mrs. Ominor clopped her book shut and rose. "I'll be only a moment. Don't leave your seats; I'll know if you do." She marched out, back straight, heels clicking.

"She won't know," Beverly muttered. "Hey, Emma, look."

Emma twisted in her seat. Atop Beverly's desk lay a mousetrap of the kind Emma had seen in the hardware store: a square of thin rods with a protruding metal tongue, and under that a small painting of a mouse in red on the flat wooden rectangle that held it all.

"Got it from my uncle's workroom," Beverly chortled. "It snaps hard, too. Ol' Ominor gets her finger caught in that, she'll know it. Go ahead and put it in her desk drawer."

"What? She'll see it!"

"Nah. Push it toward the back, just a little. When she reaches inside and touches it, *snap*!" Beverly giggled. "You'll see. It won't hurt her. Deaders don't feel anything. Go on, silly! Put it in the drawer before she comes back."

Emma felt as if she were being pulled in two directions at once. If Mrs. Ominor really didn't feel anything, it would just make her jump... but what if Bev was wrong? What if deaders *did* feel pain? "No, Bev."

Beverly's brows drew down over her nose. "Scaredy-cat!"

"No."

"You are! Teacher's pet!"

"No! Why don't *you* do it?"

"You're closer to the desk. Hurry up!"

"No!"

"You don't like deaders, do you? You want her to come and suck out your eyes?"

"Well, no, but..."

Beverly shrugged. She sat back and folded her arms over her narrow chest. "Fine. But we can't be friends any more, then."

Emma hesitated. *It's not right!* But peer pressure won. Holding the trap between thumb and forefinger, she stumbled to the desk, yanked out the drawer — it screeched like a door in a horror movie — thrust the trap in with a shaking hand, and shoved the drawer shut again with another *screeek*.

"She's coming!" Beverly hissed.

Emma scampered back to her seat and got herself settled, hands folded on the desktop, just as Mrs. Ominor opened the door and heel-clicked in.

Silence for a long, long moment as Mrs. Ominor stared first at Emma, then at Beverly. "And what is so amusing, Miss Sanders?"

"Nothing, ma'am." Beverly sounded calm.

Mrs. Ominor nodded. Without hurry she strode to the desk and pulled open the drawer (*screeek!*). Then her tall lean body seemed to slump a little, as if she were tired. She *screek*ed the drawer closed and sat in her chair.

"I've been teaching for quite a few years," she said in her metallic voice. "Did you really think I'd fall for an ancient trick like this?"

Emma swallowed.

"Come up here, both of you. Now. Stand, arms at your sides, please. Very well." Mrs. Ominor's face was smooth and hard. Emma remembered the wax figures in England that she'd seen in the Sunday paper. "Whose little idea was this?"

Silence. A glance showed Emma that Beverly's face was as blank and smooth as Mrs. Ominor's. As for herself, she wondered if the teacher could read her mind, like on those old black-and-white *Twilight Zone* shows on Channel Four.

"Tell me. Or you'll have detention every afternoon this week and next."

"It was Emma," Beverly said promptly, and Emma gaped at her.

"She brought the trap. I saw her put it in your drawer. Honest. It wasn't me."

Mrs. Ominor's green gaze was steady on her. "I see. Very well then, Miss Sanders, you may go. Miss Peters, if you'd remain a moment, please?"

Emma could not speak. The unfairness of it, the sense of betrayal, burned in her throat and eyes. Grinning, Beverly capered to her desk, grabbed her school bag, and raced out without a glance at Emma.

Mrs. Ominor pulled out the drawer and probed in it with a pencil. *Snap!* Then she reached in, drew out a red-and-white package of cigarettes, slid one white tube between her red lips, dug a lighter from her purse, and lit the cigarette. She took in a breath and expelled smoke.

"Emma," she said. "I know you didn't do it. You're not the type."

Emma whispered, "Then why'd you let her go?"

"Because staying after school doesn't *teach* her anything. I've seen too many like her. They don't learn by experience, either as children or as adults. I dread what she'll grow into, and what terrible trouble she'll give the people she meets."

"She's my friend."

"For now. Because you're useful to her.... Why did she want to do this with the trap?" Emma hesitated. "Emma, this is just between us now," and Mrs. Ominor's voice was no longer so metallic. "I won't tell your mother, or anyone else."

"She... she said the trap wouldn't hurt you. Because you're dead already."

"I see. All right. I'll tell you this once, and I want you to remember it." Mrs. Ominor took a little glass jar from her purse, unscrewed the lid, stubbed the cigarette out in it, refastened the lid, and popped the jar back into her purse.

"No, we don't feel pain," she said. "Not the way we did when we were alive. And our faces don't move, and we have to wear these, to identify us." She slid back the left sleeve of her dark green blouse. Emma saw the angry red mark carved into her teacher's forearm, a letter "D." *D is for Dead*, she thought.

"Have you noticed I don't need to breathe, except to talk or smoke?" Mrs. Ominor went on. "And we don't eat or sleep much; we do it mostly to pass the time.

"But we are not legally human. An employer doesn't need to pay us as much as he does a breather, or anything at all. We can't marry; we physically can't have children. Breathers fear us and avoid us. And by law, we can live only in certain designated places."

"Like that church on Rampart?" Emma whispered. She'd seen it, a high-walled place like pictures of old castles in the *Little Golden Books*.

"That's right."

"Do you... do you get old and die? I mean, for good?"

"We don't seem to age. But the Change that remade the world and made it possible for us to come back, it's so new that nobody knows how long we'll exist, or how we'll stop."

"I don't get it."

"Emma... how can I put this? Animals die, like your hamster you told about in class. People die. But none of them knows *when* it will happen."

Mrs. Ominor's voice was strangely soft. Emma wondered in a burst of almost-adult clarity whether her teacher would have smiled if she could have.

"Neither do we," Mrs. Ominor said. "Which demonstrates God's mercy... and, I think, makes us as human as you." She picked up her book and opened it. "You may go, Emma. Be sure to do Chapter Six in your reader for tomorrow."

For a long time that afternoon, Emma sat in her room, cuddling Mrs. Renfro. She even turned down an offer of some milk and cookies, so that her mother checked Emma's forehead "to see if you have a fever." At last she went away and left Emma to replay the sounds and pictures that flashed through her brain.

Deaders don't feel anything... They hate us.

I think that makes us as human as you.

Emma came out of a daze to hear the front door open. She had forgotten it was Daddy's night to have dinner with them. She settled Mrs. Renfro against a pillow and scurried out.

As Emma raced down the hall, Daddy was hanging up his suit coat and loosening his tie. Mommy trotted out of the kitchen and they kissed. After hearing from Bev and other girls how their parents screamed and fought, Emma realized how lucky she was that her parents loved each other, and her. "Dinner in ten minutes, Bob."

"Sounds good. I see you have a small sergeant-major here to make sure I wash up before dinner." He patted Emma's head, unsmilingly as usual. He unbuttoned his shirt cuffs and began to roll up his sleeves. Two precise turns of the right sleeve, two of the left.

The left...

Emma became aware that Daddy had said something. "What was that, Daddy?"

"You're in another world tonight, hon. Did you do all right in school today?"

Emma drew in a long breath. For an instant she felt as if every piece of furniture in the room, the chair and sofa and tables she'd known all her life, had shifted their places. But when she looked, they were where they'd always been.

"Sure, Daddy," she said. "School is sort of fun, I guess. Can I bring Mrs. Renfro to eat with us?"

The next morning Emma Peters strode, her school bag swinging at her side, through the front door of her school, through the auditorium, and out into the rear yard. There were still a few minutes before the first bell rang, and the early arrivals in first and second grade were running and shouting and playing games.

Emma marched over to where Beverly knelt with two other girls, absorbed in a game of jacks. "Beverly," she said.

Beverly scowled up at her. "What is it?"

"Got to talk to you for a second."

Sighing, Beverly rose to her feet. Today she wore a bright white dress and glossy black shoes, the same shoes, Emma thought, she'd worn when she killed the bluebird. "I'm playing here. What is it?"

Emma set down her school bag. "This," she said.

She lifted her arms and slammed them into Beverly's chest with all her force. The other girl shrieked and windmilled her arms. She toppled straight back and landed with a squelch in the mud puddle that never seemed to dry up. Dazed, she sat blinking up at Emma. Her hands were plastered with mud, and when she wiped her face a new splotch appeared on her cheek. That white dress, Emma thought with satisfaction, looked like Beverly had been playing in chocolate pudding.

"Why'd you do that?" Beverly squalled.

Emma shouted back:

"Because I don't like you, Beverly Sanders, and we're not friends any more! And I don't care if Mrs. Ominor's a deader! You hear me? *I like her and I DON'T CARE!*"

The boys and girls in the yard began to laugh and point, not at Emma but at the furious Beverly, who was trying to roll out of the mud. Over the laughter Emma heard the rapid footsteps of Mrs. Thames, who was yard monitor this week, bearing down on her.

Detention again, Emma thought, but with a kind of happy wildness that told her she had done the right thing. *And I don't care about that either....*

THE DRAGON DETECTOR

ELANA GOMEL

The call came at 3:40 pm and woke me up. Afternoon is the worst time of day. It is sandwiched between the morning when everything seems fresh and ripe with promise, and the evening when darkness gives you a decent pretext for going to bed. In the afternoon the sky is glassy, the sun merciless, and you feel passage of wasted time as physically as bleeding.

The call was from Rose of course, though she used another anonymous number. But who else would be calling me? David only did when there was some loose end of the divorce business to settle and Cassie....

"SFO," said Rose's clipped voice in my ear. "Third terminal."

I savored the burst of adrenaline. Unfortunately I am immune to substance abuse. Alcohol passes through my body like water; pot gives me migraines; the antidepressants that I had been prescribed after the divorce had all the efficacy of sugar pills. My brain, with its "unique and precious software" as Rose put it, serves the state's interests well. It does nothing for me.

I drove to the airport in my new SUV. Pale sunshine oozed down my windshield, curdled by the grit in the air. The Vacaville fire-dragon had been bad. Half of the town was smoking ruins by the time the dragon collapsed in upon itself, tunneling into a point of nothingness above the charred ground.

It was not my fault, I kept telling myself. Too bad I cannot not get addicted even to self-deception.

The traffic was light, so I got to SFO in record time. They were waiting for me: Rose and two of her interchangeable goons. I could never fix their faces in my memory. They all blended into one generic image like a stock photo: a thick neck, a crewcut, and a blank stare. I am not good at face recognition. I am not good at anything, except the one thing that makes me indispensable.

The goons took care of my parking and escorted me through the chaos of the airport, parting the crowds like twin avatars of Moses marching through the Red Sea. And if this was not enough to assure me of my importance, Rose Delano, the FBI director herself, was limping by my side.

It turned out to be a new eatery, called Farm-something or other and featuring all-organic salads, gluten-free sandwiches, and Napa wines. I was glad it was not a luggage carousel. Nothing is worse than standing by the hypnotically floating succession of identical suit-cases, peering at their scuffed leather and waiting for the sharp crack of a hatching.

The eatery had been evacuated. I stepped over the yellow tape. Rose moved to follow me, her scrunched-up body in a ridiculously formal black suit hovering over the tape like a crow. I shook my head and she stepped back. It was not to protect her. If the dragon hatched before I located the egg, a couple of extra yards would not make any difference. At the end of the day, the entire San Francisco International Airport could be a wilderness of ashes or a swamp overflowing with pungent slime. But I needed to be alone when I was working. Other people were a distraction to me – as David had never failed to point out.

I stopped in the middle of the eatery, taking it all in: the lifeless fluorescent glare; the abandoned plastic plates, overflowing with dying vegetables and dead meat; the xylophone of multicolored sodas in the fridge; the bulging shapes of wine bottles like a row of portly Victorian gentlemen ...When I *look*, I need to empty out my mind. I need to be fully present in the moment – not second-guessing myself, not figuring out, not thinking at all – just *looking*. Perhaps that was why I failed, time and again, to train a successor. How could I explain my "method" when there was no method at all?

But I could see nothing except for the flotsam of transient lives. Panic welled up in my throat.

I glanced back at Rose. Her reconstructed face was not made for expressing emotions but I knew she was frightened. We were standing near a hand-grenade with a lit fuse.

I squinted at the salad bar under the sloping glass cover. The colors were smudged somehow: the red ripeness of tomatoes clotting into maroon; the cheerful green of arugula deepened into somber sage...It looked strange but then I realized it was because the glass of the case was oily, painted with swirls of fatty deposits. I went back staring at the wine bottles, their uniform darkness promising some secret locked inside, even though I knew it was dangerous to succumb to the obvious symbolism of everyday life.

Behind me, I heard the tapping of Rose's high-heeled shoe on the floor.

Rose was not born with a curved spine and a shiny plastic mask for a face. The Orlando dragon, one of the first ones to evolve beyond the simplicity of fire- and smoke-drakes, had made her what she was now. There had been so many more since then: water-dragons, to poison rivers and make the Caspian Sea into a giant reservoir of acid; flesh-dragons, to breed swarms of flying leeches that burrowed into the bodies of the victims; slime-dragons, to vomit forth waves of suffocating, greasy foam...

Grease! I sprinted toward the salad bar, ran my hand over the glass and felt it give, stickily, like a liquefying corpse.

"This!" I yelled, pointing to the bar.

The agents moved with a lightning speed and I just managed to flop down and roll out of the way as a hailstorm of bullets shattered the case. The noise was deafening but still could not drown the screams in the terminal. I wondered how many people would be prevented by PTSD from ever entering an airport again. Carbon taxes had failed to stem the flow of air traffic; perhaps dragons would. I assumed that this was the terrorists' calculus.

The rattle of bullets died down and I risked raising my head. The pseudo-farm looked like it was growing broken glass instead of produce. Streams of wine and rivulets of soda mingled in a complicated beverage delta on the floor. But my eyes were instantly drawn to a smashed tray that used to hold quinoa salad and I felt the tension drain out of my body.

The tray was swollen and puffy. The scattered grains of quinoa, inflated to the size of a ball bearing, quivered, jelly-like. And from a pile of chopped vegetables, a single curved talon, as big as my hand, stuck out.

I was right. That had been the dragon egg.

I waited for Cassie to call until I could plausibly lie to myself that it was too late and she was already in bed. Of course, I knew she was probably chatting with her girlfriends on the phone. David never insisted on reasonable hours. Nevertheless, I was a bad mother. He was a stay-at-home dad, a perfect parent. The fact that it was my money that made it possible for him to go freelance, while having full custody, was irrelevant.

I could call or text Cassie myself... to have my call rejected and my text go unanswered. And then tomorrow there would be a brief impersonal response, and behind it I could hear David's mildly reproachful voice, saying, "Cas, she is your mum!" and Cassie's resentful grunt. So I went to bed. Not to sleep – I would doze off after midnight if I was lucky – but to feel safe and protected in my cocoon. I had piled up old books on the other side of the bed where David used to sleep. I turned on the TV. Surrounded by books and fragrant candles, I could cope with the state of the world. Sometimes I thought it would be nice to have a pet but I was allergic to cats. As for dogs... one of the first eggs I had discovered was in a sweet little Chihuahua.

The discovery of a dragon egg at SFO was not on top of the news-cast. Unsurprising, considering what was. A dragon had hatched in the Old City of Basel in Switzerland. The newsfeed showed shell-shocked people staring pleadingly into the camera as if expecting to see the faces of their lost loved ones on the other side of the screen. A giant Catherine wheel was sagging over the demolished cathedral; a 700-year-old bridge was reduced to a path of rubble across the shallow Rhine. It had been a stone drake, a heavy lumbering beast, shedding rocks as it worked its way through the Marketplatz crowds.

I turned the TV off and lay on my back, staring at the ceiling dappled with writhing shadows from the candles. The sales of home candles and decorative lights had gone down because people mistak-enly associated them with fire-drakes. In fact, dragon eggs could be placed in any object, and there was no apparent connection between the incubator and the type of dragon that hatched from it. You played Russian roulette when you bought a loaf of bread, a grandfather clock, or a pet rabbit.

But not me. A hatched dragon could not be killed; it simply collapsed into nothingness when its brief lifetime had run its course. But before the hatching, the egg could be destroyed. And I was the only one who could see an egg inside its everyday disguise.

A gust of wind rattled the windowpane. I knew I was under constant surveillance, which did not bother me. Pathetically, it provided a sense of company. After the divorce, I found out all my friends had been David's. My parents were dead. I was a pathological loner and it made Rose's job much easier. She did not have to worry about a visitor planting an egg in my dishwasher or sofa. A terrorist had to be on the scene physically to do whatever they did to turn an everyday object into a monster incubator.

Nobody knew what it was. Rose would undoubtedly administer any kind of torture to a terrorist to find out the secret of sowing dragon eggs, the Geneva Convention be damned. But there had never been a terrorist captured alive. All of them had eggs nesting in their bodies, and attempting to arrest them would merely loose yet another nasty indestructible beast.

The White House and most of Washington DC had closed to all visitors. But you cannot fence in airports, malls or streets. Or National Parks. Or a random stretch of public land. The last wood dragon that hatched in the Bay Area turned a neighborhood's favorite hiking trail into a palisade of sharpened sticks where joggers and dog-walkers hung, impaled.

The FBI received tips, of course; this was how Rose had known about SFO. But she never told me about her sources and my timid attempts at asking questions were met with silence. I was just a useful tool. A human-shaped dragon detector.

Cassie called me when I was in the supermarket. When I saw my daughter's face on the screen, I dropped a package of frozen peas onto the floor and lunged toward a quiet corner.

"Hi, mum!" That word sat awkwardly on her lips whose shape had changed since the last time I saw her. They were fuller and rosier.

Cassie is beautiful. I am not. But there has never been any resentment on my side. Maybe it is because I do not think of myself as a woman. I am a little sexless scarecrow hiding in the corner. I am a weird geek with pale eyes and thin mousy hair. I am Ash.

Cassie takes after her father, whose courtship of me was one of those inexplicable miracles that only come once in a lifetime. I was lucky; I had two of them.

"Hi, darling!" I said too chirpily. "How are you? How is school?"

Her face clouded over and I berated myself. Here I was, squandering this rare and precious opportunity by nagging!

"School is OK," she said vaguely. "Hey, mum, can we meet today?"

At first I thought I had misheard. Initially Cassie was to spend every second weekend with me but after a year of my being constantly called away, David had convinced me that Cassie was better off without being jerked between two homes. "She needs stability in her life," he had said in that soothing voice whose magic did not fade even after the divorce. "It's a vulnerable age, and she has already been through so much..." He did not need to finish that sentence. I agreed.

Since then I only talked to Cassie when David, always conscientious, urged her to phone me. I was screwing up my courage to negotiate an overnight stay at Thanksgiving but it was two months away. And here she was, asking me for a meeting!

"Of course, darling!" I said, hoping she could not hear the choking in my voice. "Anytime."

I barely recognized my daughter.

Not because she had grown – that was expected. Not because she was even more beautiful than before – I had seen it even through the smudged glass of my phone. But because there was now an edge to this beauty, a strange febrile glow. She seemed to leave a trail of sparks as she walked into the Peet's. Heads turned.

I felt as if our roles had suddenly switched as if I was an awkward and insecure teenager, about to be rebuked by a stern parent.

I asked if she wanted a Coke.

"Water," she said.

She drank slowly while I raked my brain trying to guess what she could possibly want from me that she could not get from her father. Finally I hit on one plausible explanation: that she was pregnant. I was ashamed to realize that it cheered me up; at least, she would need me for something.

But when Cassie finally spoke, it had nothing to do with a visit to Planned Parenthood.

"Mum," she asked, "can you teach somebody else to become a dragon detector?"

I choked on my stewed tea.

"You know I can't talk about it!"

My daughter's luminous green eyes she had not inherited from me did not leave my face, and my resolve melted away.

"No," I said truthfully. "I can't teach anybody. I don't think it can be taught."

"So what is it?"

"It's... it's like an inborn talent. Hereditary."

And then I saw it.

"No!" I yelled so loudly that a couple of patrons turned their heads in my direction. "No," I repeated, lowering my voice to an agitated hiss. "Don't even think about it! You don't have it!"

"How do you know?"

"Because... because..." I cast around, feeling lost because *how* did I know it? "Because you're not like me. We are different."

"But I am your daughter!"

"Yes," I said. "You are my daughter. And I'd know if you had my... my talent. But I'm pretty sure you don't. I knew I had it since I was six. You are sixteen."

"But there were no dragons when you were six, were there?"

"No," I said, "there were no dragons. The Children of Gaia got active when you were about ten. But I knew I had a special sight. I could find lost objects and see into locked safe-boxes, that kind of things. My parents suspected I would become a stage magician and were horrified."

That elicited a wan smile from her.

I was about to launch into the safe waters of childhood recollections when Cassie, once again, steered our conversation in an unexpected direction:

"What did you think when it started? The Children of Gaia?"

I shrugged.

"What could I think? The same as any rational person on the planet: they are crazy and evil."

"Even though they are saying they try to prevent a catastrophe?"

"That's what all terrorists say. Whatever they are fighting against is the greatest evil... blah-blah. And then they kill a bunch of innocent people. Even if they manage to achieve their goal, they'll turn out to be worse than whoever or whatever they are trying to overthrow."

"How can anything be worse than the extinction of life on Earth?"

I blinked. Did my daughter really come to meet me in order to discuss politics? I had steeled myself for *the* question that had blighted our relationship. I had weighed and discarded various answers:

I did not really leave you...

It was Dad's decision too, not mine alone.

We were trying to do what was best for you.

Anything but confessing the humiliating truth: that when David told me he did not love me anymore I went to pieces. I could not pull myself together enough to care for my daughter. And when I finally crawled out from under the pall of depression, it was too late: the divorce agreement had been signed and Cassie, sullen and dry-eyed, moved into her dad's new house.

But this? Was she baiting me? When I was her age, radical ecology had been a thing and hip teenagers talked about "curing the planet from the disease of humanity." But since the dragon attacks started, the public opinion had undergone a shift. To talk about climate change was to side with the dragon sowers, and nobody wanted to be suspected as a sympathizer.

"That's what their manifestoes say," I said. "Who knows if they are for real? No terrorist has even been apprehended, so maybe it's a bunch of crap. Maybe they are just having fun killing people."

"Fun? Sacrificing themselves in the process?"

This finally got my goat.

"Fanatics don't value their own lives because they don't value other people's lives," I said, more sharply than I intended. "And if I were you, Cassie, I would give it a rest. After Basel, people won't appreciate theoretical debates about the ethics of mass murder!"

I expected an angry retort but she just stared into her empty glass. Her phone pinged; she glanced at it and rose to her feet.

"Got to go," she said.

I got up too, longing to hug her but afraid of rejection. And then another miracle happened: she lunged forward and put her arms around me.

"It was good to see you, mum," she mumbled into my sweater.

"It was good to see you too, sweetie," I managed to whisper. "Maybe we can do it again soon."

Cassie stepped back and I saw a tear crawl down her cheek.

"Maybe," she said and was out of the coffee-shop before I could find anything else to say. But it did not matter. I walked on clouds as I went back to my car.

My daughter cried because she was parting from me!

The rest of the day went by in a happy glow. I fantasized about mending the fences with Cassie, having her come over, stay overnight, perhaps eventually moving in with me...

Rose called just before bedtime. Her glistening mask of a face filled the screen. The Orlando dragon had spat jets of organic acid that literally melted the flesh off her bones.

"Ashley," she said and fell silent. I waited, resentful that she was intruding on my bliss but also feeling the first stirrings of excitement.

"There has been a...tip."

"Where?" I asked. Rose's unwonted hesitation seemed to indicate that my next assignment involved long-distance flying. She knew I hated planes.

"It's about you."

"Me?"

"We received information that there may be an assassination attempt."

It took a moment for this to sink in.

"I am the target?"

"Yes."

The phone almost slipped out of my sweat-slicked hand.

"What are you going to do?"

"There are already agents around your house, so don't worry, nobody can get in. But I think it's not enough. You are unique. Irreplaceable. We need to move you to a safe location."

I groaned, looking at the familiar mess of my bedroom and feeling like a snail about to be yanked out of her shell.

"Where?"

"I'd rather not say. The line is encrypted but still.... Anyway, you have about ten minutes to pack."

My protests sounded unconvincing even to myself and Rose paid them no attention. With a sigh, I walked to the bathroom to select the necessary toiletries. I clicked on the light and met my own eyes in the mirror.

Pale writhing flames wormed their way through the tunnels of my pupils.

I caught myself on the edge of the sink, pressing my face into the glass, telling myself it was an illusion, or an incipient migraine, or a brain tumor. But I knew. I was the dragon detector. The one and only. I saw hatching dragons as they grew in wood, stone, or flesh.

A dragon was growing in me. Somebody had planted an egg in my body. And there was no mystery about who it had been.

I stumbled back to the bedroom. The strange thing was that there were no strange sensations. I had seen the dragon inside myself but I had not felt it yet. Not as I had felt my daughter growing inside me, announcing her eventual arrival with morning sickness, bloat and baby kicks. My daughter, a sweet little monster feeding on my blood.

Cassie had been recruited by the terrorists. Did she truly believe that killing her mother was the way to save Mother Earth? Was she a sociopath? A resentful little bitch? Was she trying to pay me back for abandoning her?

What did I know about her? What do parents know about their children?

I pulled the drawer of my bedside table and there it was, a sleek little gun Rose had given me and insisted I learn how to use.

Once a dragon egg is implanted in a living body, it has to hatch unless the body is destroyed. There is no way to cut it out. But I still had some time before a beast clawed its way out of me, unfurled it leathery wings or stretched its scaly appendages, and rained fire, or spat acid, or trampled cities. Would some remnant of myself survive in the monster? Would I delight in making others suffer as I suffered?

I still had enough time to pick up my phone and call Rose. Enough to tell her David's address.

No terrorist had ever been apprehended but even one arrest could start unraveling the whole organization of the Children of Gaia. If they came upon her suddenly, put her under sedation... The terrorists must have some way to delay or even neutralize the hatching of a dragon egg. After all, in previous attempts to capture a suspect alive, they would hatch their egg instantly, while having gone through months and maybe years with it lying dormant in their bodies.

Perhaps Cassie knew the secret. Perhaps there was still hope for me.

But none for Cassie. She would be arrested, interrogated, and executed. The new Defense of Humanity Act gave extraordinary powers to the security services.

Cassie. A sower of dragons. A terrorist. A would-be matricide.

My daughter.

I lifted the gun and clicked the safety off.

There is only one way to kill a dragon. Destroy its egg.

I pressed the muzzle to my forehead.

THE LAKE COTTAGE

MICHELLE F GODDARD

I remember the day I drowned. My mom screaming from the beach, high-pitched whines, interrupted by a whoosh and then the undulating groan of the water as I went under. Mom's screams becoming shorter and sharper. The groan longer and louder. My heart beating in my chest, madly at first but then slower; a flame snuffed out by water.

The fact that I didn't die, doesn't mean I didn't drown. Saying I almost drowned feels disingenuous. I drowned. I went under. I sank. Down. Deeper. The cold, more than the icy depth trenched by a glacier millions of years ago, but a force that made my arms alien and ungainly. The dark more than the silt and mud that murked the water grey, but a shroud that hid your feet at the end of your legs.

But when I looked across to Nadine, sitting in the passenger's seat of my car, I couldn't say that. I had learned that much at least.

"So I may as well tell you before my mom does. I almost drowned at that lake."

Nadine's eyes grew wide. "Oh?"

"So don't be surprised if she tries to convince you that you shouldn't go. I mean, don't take it personally."

"I won't. I suppose that sort of thing can be traumatic," Nadine said, giving my leg a squeeze. "Watching your youngest sink below the water…"

"Yeah. Traumatic."

At the time, I didn't know which was worse; the screaming from the beach, or the screaming from behind their closed bedroom door.

"I don't care how good a deal you got for this place," my mother had said. The door flung open and my parents stood staring at me. My mother recovered first. "What are you doing here? You're supposed to be resting." She turned me around and guided me back to my bed.

The last thing I had wanted was to be alone in my bedroom. But my mother wasn't interested in what I wanted. If I had had my way, I would have spent the evening sitting on the dock and staring out at the lake. Searching.

Beside me, Nadine shifted in the passenger's seat and pulled down the hem of her dress.

"You didn't have to buy a dress for this," I said.

"You do realize chasing after a classroom of five-year-olds does not lend itself to having pretty clothes. As it is, I had to borrow these shoes."

"Well, everything looks great. You look great."

Nadine leaned back into her seat and gave me a sideways glance that made my heart leap about. "Just don't get used to this."

"Once in a while isn't so bad."

"Sure. As long as I don't have to do anything useful. Like walking. I think I've already gotten a blister. These are definitely sitting-down shoes."

"Is that a brand?"

"You're cute."

We found the closest parking lot to the restaurant my mother had chosen, but it was still a bit of a walk. Nadine put on a brave face, but I heard her sigh when she sat down. A last-minute call from my mother had indicated we should go on and eat without her. Typical. But I couldn't lie; I was a little relieved. My mother was more agreeable, taken in small doses.

We had just finished eating when my mother arrived. With a slight wince, Nadine rose to her feet to greet her. I worried that blister was the least of her worries as my mother visibly sized her up.

"So. You're Nadine," my mother said as we all sat down. "John, I don't know how you manage to find such pretty girls in your line of work."

"He was working on a house near my school," Nadine said. "One thing led to another."

"A schoolteacher. With those shoes? On your salary?"

"Mom," I said, with a voice I could not help be ice-rimmed.

"Not hardly," Nadine said with a laugh. "And are they shoes or torture devices? Am I right?"

My mother smiled, but her eyes didn't warm in the least.

"I understand you're a decorator," Nadine said. "I would have loved to see your apartment. John tells me it's lovely."

"That's why I suggested the restaurant. I'm having it redone."

"Again?" I asked.

"Out with the old," my mother said, her eyes never leaving

Nadine's face. "I'm surprised John would have anything to say about my work."

"He's very proud," Nadine said.

"Is he? Funny, as he abandoned me to go live with his father."

"You make it sound like you were all alone," I said. "You had Peter."

"If you'll excuse me," Nadine said rising to her feet. "I'm just going to powder my nose." She gave me a smile as she reached for my hand to give it a squeeze. "And it seems you two have some things to talk about."

"She's certainly forward," my mother said, as Nadine headed toward the Ladies.

"I like that about her. You know where you stand with Nadine."

"Do you. Well, I can tell you two are nothing alike. Certainly too different to make a good match."

"You've spent all of ten minutes with her."

"I'm just looking out for you, John. Look what happened to me and your father."

"And on that note," I said, "I wanted to ask you about a ring. I guess it would have been your engagement ring."

"That old thing?"

"I always thought it was pretty and I thought it would be perfect for Nadine."

"Really? You're there with her?"

"Maybe. I think so. Yes. I went shopping but I could never find anything as nice, and since you obviously don't wear it, I thought you would give it to me."

"You're welcome to it, but I don't have it. I don't know what happened to it. Maybe Peter has it."

"He doesn't."

"Well then, I must have lost it."

I flashed back to the last time I remember my mother being at the lake. Another argument. Not the worst, but there was a finality to it that I only now recognize for what it was. My father, still in a cast from falling off the cottage roof. My mother, not at all dressed for the woods, in a pants suit and white stiff-necked collar, looking official. I had wondered how she managed to walk out to the end of the dock in her high-heeled shoes; the one time she didn't stagger and jerk, jostled by the water as if it were trying to shake her off.

"Now enough of that, John," my mother said, breaking me out of my thoughts. "This is supposed to be a pleasant visit. And your fiancée is returning from the bathroom."

"Please don't say anything about the ring. I haven't asked Nadine yet."

My mother locked her lips with a pretend key and gave me a wink just as I heard Nadine's tentative steps behind me.

"So," my mother said as Nadine sat down. "Has John told you about the lake?"

"About him drowning?" Nadine said. "Yes."

"And that's all?"

"All?"

"John, don't you think she has a right to know what she's in for? Especially if—"

"Mom."

"If what?" Nadine asked.

"If you're planning on staying," my mother said. "How long *were* you planning on staying? At the cottage."

"I'm a teacher. So my summer vacation has just begun. I'll stay as long as we can, I suppose. John has got some jobs on the go. He'll have to check on them, I'm sure. But he's got a great crew—"

"And leave you there by yourself? John, don't you dare."

"I wasn't planning on leaving her alone."

"I'd be fine by myself," Nadine said, her gaze darting between us.

"No," my mother said, her face cold and stern. "You would not."

"Are there bears?" Nadine said, with a nervous laugh. "Cougars? Wolves? I've heard that's possible that far north."

"Nothing so mundane, my dear," my mother said. "That place is cursed. The real danger is that lake. I told John's father but he didn't want to listen. All he'd ever say was if we don't trouble the waters, they won't trouble us. The trouble was, he valued that cottage more than our marriage."

"That's not how I saw it," I said.

"You were a child and you always took his side."

I leaned back from the table and gave Nadine a tight and completely ineffective smile. "So much for a pleasant visit, eh?"

Again, Nadine reached for me, her fingertips resting lightly on mine as if I was a bird that might fly away. My mother's gaze flew to our touching hands and wilted, but when she looked away, it was metal bright.

"Don't worry about it, Nadine," my mother said. "Things always deteriorate into hard feelings, when that lake cottage becomes a topic of conversation. You'll see."

"I suppose I don't handle it as well as Peter," I said.

"Peter and I don't waste time discussing it. Did you hear, he's about to make partner at his firm?"

Once onto safer ground, my mother played nice for the next hour as we lingered over dessert and coffee and tip-toed around the land-mines of my childhood.

It was only when we got back into the car, did my jaw unclench. I massaged the last of the tension away as I waited for Nadine to pack her dress and shoes. I had already changed into cottage attire.

"That's better," she said, as she slid into the car. "Though this blister isn't going to forgive me anytime soon. Speaking of forgive-ness, your mother still seems bitter about the divorce. And she seri-ously hates that lake."

"Understatement," I said, as I pulled out of the parking spot. We entered downtown traffic and began to inch our way east through the city. "She hates it like it was a mistress."

"Your parents didn't divorce over a cottage."

"But it was their favourite argument."

"Let me guess. She wanted a time-share in Florida."

"Pretty much."

"I just don't get those. Basically, you pack up all your stuff, put them in the car, drive for 'x' amount of miles, only to unpack it all to do exactly what you would have done if you had stayed at home."

"Exactly. The perfect vacation. According to Mom and Peter. I don't know. Maybe if I hadn't drowned, things would have been different."

"Did you drown on purpose?"

"It was my fault. I wanted to keep up with Peter. I shouldn't have been swimming out that far."

"And he saved you?"

I shrugged, hiding the shudder that always accompanied the memory. Panic succumbing to the dark and the cold, slowly distilling into a thick embrace. Then something touching me. I felt myself pushed and pulled. Dark eyes stared at me through the water, then slid away as I shot upwards towards light.

"What?" Nadine asked. "What saved you?"

"Adrenalin. I guess. I found myself above the water and near enough to the shore to stand."

Nadine slowly nodded and then blew air through her lips. "That can happen. I was on a trip with a school bus once. Some kid went into anaphylactic shock. He was, what, eighty pounds soaking wet? Oh my god. It took two gym teachers and a father to hold him down so that we could administer his epi-pen. Fear can make you strong. You're lucky fear didn't just make you give up. I almost didn't go on the school trip this year, remembering that incident."

"But you went. Fear didn't stop you," I said, fighting against the urge to make the sentence rise into a hopeful question.

"It was Ottawa," Nadine said, giving me a wry look. "Have you ever seen Ottawa in the spring? It's beautiful."

"Well, it's not spring but we could go there now. Stay at a nice hotel? Art galleries? Byward Market? Or we could head straight on to Montreal?"

"Are you trying to get out of this? Did I do something wrong?"

"Wrong? Hell no. Wearing those shoes, I think you took one for the team."

"Well then, what's all this talk about?"

"The lake isn't for everyone." I laughed and leaned back against the seat, wearing cavalier like it was Kevlar. "Just giving you an out."

"Maybe I don't want out." I felt Nadine's hand on my cheek. "It'll be better once we're out of the centre core."

I spared a glance toward her and held her warm gaze against the chill of my worry, as I turned back to the traffic around me.

Nadine was right. We passed the city limits and I felt a weight come off my chest.

"So," Nadine said, shifting to stare at me as I drove. "Your mom seemed to hint that there was more to this lake cottage? Tell me more about this curse."

"She thought it was cursed because nothing seemed to turn out the way she wanted. We'd want to expand, and we'd have permit issues. Her designs would not comply with the rules, when the building inspector would discover some hidden water source right where she wanted to build. It got so she thought the water was purposefully deviating to screw with her."

"Seriously?" Nadine said with a chuckle.

"She'd want to repaint the wood trim, yet no matter how well she'd prep the surface, it would bubble and peel. It got so weird that only I or my dad could do the dishes. Anytime she tried, the water shot out of the faucet looking dark and smelling sulphurous."

"There's nothing wrong with water that smells a little eggy."

"My mom took it personally. She refused to swim in the lake and had my dad bring jugs of water for her, even though we had a perfectly good well. That is, when she stayed at the cottage at all."

"And you? Never had any issues with the water? Even with almost drowning?"

I almost corrected her. I *had* drowned. I felt as if I had coughed up half the lake when I broke the surface, chilled and numb and dizzy. I had staggered toward the shore, the water churning around me as my parents and brother ran to me, their murmurs of concern and relief as distant as wind through trees. My father took me in his arms and I rested my head on his shoulder as I looked back toward the water. Out where the lake was still, a bump lay on the surface and two eyes stared back at me. I raised my hand toward it, and with a splash, it disappeared beneath the water.

"No," I said, with a soft smile. "I never had a fear of that lake. I loved it up there. Though, I think for my mother, that felt like a betrayal."

"What does Peter think about all this?"

"I don't think he's been up in years. Not since we were kids. Summers were at the cottage, but when Peter visited us there, he would spend the entire time in his room with a book, or online, if he could get online. Oh yeah, and we might not be able to get online."

"Oh, no. What will become of us."

"Laugh now. Let's see what happens when you go into cellphone withdrawal."

"I'm hoping you'll distract me," she said, with a heavy-lidded look that made me stare at her a little too long for road safety.

"I've got a telescope," I said. "No city lights up there. Nothing but the moon and stars. Great for star-gazing."

"That sounds wonderful, too."

I smiled at Nadine but turned away as my happiness dipped. What would Nadine feel about that dark water? What would she say if I told her about eyes that watched from the lake? Would she laugh, or scoff? Would how I feel about the place, end up a betrayal?

Nadine reached over, turned on the radio and began searching through the dials. Conversation slid away from my parents and their divorce and the lake cottage, and I was happy to let it go, unsure how to proceed. For the next while, we drove through easy silences, interspersed with comments on the scenery and detours onto other benign topics.

We had passed the three-quarter mark of our trip. I heard Nadine hiss in pain and looked over to find her wincing and staring at her heel.

"You okay?" I asked.

"I bumped it when I shifted in my seat. I'm not used to this much sitting."

"Let me see," I said, with a nod at her foot.

Nadine brought her foot up to rest on her knee. Her blister had expanded to the full width of her heel, and bulged, red-rimmed and angry.

"Should you pop that?" I asked. "We could stop at a pharmacy."

"No. But I do have to pee."

I pulled into the next gas station. It was one of those that rang a little bell as you drove in and had a gas-station attendant, an old guy in coveralls who limped out to greet us with a smile.

Nadine got out of the car. "Washroom?" The attendant pointed. "Thanks." She stretched as she headed for the restroom sign.

"What'll it be?" The attendant asked.

"Fill'er up," I said.

Nadine returned as the attendant finished cleaning the windows. "So are we in the country yet?" Nadine asked.

"Any more country and you'd be out in the bush," the old gas-station attendant said. "No place for a city girl like you. You've got a blister from sitting-down shoes, my wife calls them."

Nadine looked at me and raised her eyebrows. "There's a husband in the know."

"Oh, give him time," the old man said, with a wide grin. "These things take time. Time and conversation. You newlyweds are always in such a hurry."

"Oh, we're not newlyweds," Nadine said. "And I'm not a city girl. Not really."

The old guy squinted down at her foot. "That's a pretty nasty blister."

"This was a momentary lapse in good judgement. But the fresh air is clearing my head." She turned her foot to look at her heel. "And I imagine some healthy living up at the lake will see to this."

In moments we were back on the road.

"That blister does look bad," I said. "I don't know if I like the idea of you running around some old cottage. You're looking for an infection."

"Things have to come out in their own time. But they always come out." She stretched and settled deeper into her seat. "And it looks worse than it feels. The air really does help. It's much cooler here than in the city."

"In the winter, the lake freezes solid. It's almost easier to get across in February than it is in April."

"Why's that?"

"Drive to the point and walk right across. Some skidoo. And there are no bugs in the winter."

"Wimp."

"Let's see you say that next year, when we open the cottage for May two-four weekend."

"Oh? And will I be coming up next May?"

I shrugged and grinned and hoped my heart wasn't beating as loudly outside of my chest as it was in my own ears.

"Wow," Nadine said. "Making plans with me almost a year in

advance. That's gutsy."

She smiled at me and though I returned her smile, I couldn't keep eye contact. I think if I had had my mother's ring, I might have been tempted to pull over and propose right then. Instead, I pretended to become suddenly concerned with my speed and imagined potholes in the road. That was safer than the uncharted territory of my heart. She had met my mother and not run. But she hadn't yet met my father. And if I was being honest, she hadn't seen the lake and the cottage, and I needed her to see it.

An hour later, we sat in a coffee shop, my father like my mother preferring to meet in a public place. Nadine had plucked a regional real-estate paper from the stand near the door and was flipping through the pages. "It's amazing what you can get north of here for not a lot of money."

"Sure, if you're prepared to stay isolated for the entire winter. The snow plows don't always come when you want them."

"I guess. But seeing these prices and knowing what a house costs in the burbs... it's just staggering."

"You pay in other ways. Stuff you take for granted, you can't here."

"For instance."

"Getting work done on your cottage. Not a lot of contractors would come out this far and those who do are pretty busy. Over the years my dad got better at doing small jobs but he was never very talented with his hands, much to my mother's disappointment. Of course, once my mom was out of the picture, there wasn't as much pressure to work on the place."

"A real bachelor pad?"

"A man-cave, thank you very much."

"And that's being kind," my father said as he limped toward the table.

"Dad," I said, standing to pull out his chair.

He hung his cane on the back before easing himself down. "Good to see you, John."

"Dad, this is Nadine."

"Thanks for dropping in to see me on the way to the cottage," my dad said.

"Of course," Nadine said.

"I'd like to get out there. Soak in the water. Always used to make me feel better. Healing properties in that water."

"Then why don't you?" Nadine asked.

"My arthritis has been acting up something fierce. And those stairs up to the front door were always tricky. Lately even more so. All I'd need is to fall. No one might find me 'til next spring."

"Don't say that, Dad."

"Just a joke. What isn't a joke is the notice I received. This might be your first and last trip up to the lake. I'm going to be selling the cottage."

"What?" I said. "Why?"

"I guess the township wants to fancy up Main Street and they're looking to fill their coffers. My property taxes are going up. Considerably. I don't know how I'm going to pay it."

"Did you talk to Peter about it?" I asked. "He could help get your finances in order at least. Or maybe give you a loan. He's got the money."

"I won't ask that from him. From either of my sons. I know you're just starting up. New businesses take time to get on their feet. This is my problem. Not yours."

"But, Dad—"

"And Peter doesn't want anything to do with the cottage. He's made that clear. He actually told me to write him out of my will. Not that there's much, other than the cottage. So I guess it'll be your headache, if I don't sell it. But the way things are, selling it might be my only option. And a kindness to you. Maybe that place wasn't such a good deal. I mean look what it's cost me."

"It can't be that bad, Dad."

"I don't know. Your mother always said the place was cursed. The water pump has been acting dodgy, we might need to replace the wood stove. Or maybe it's the chimney pipe. I don't know. But the last time I tried a fire, it smoked me out. Can't get the place to warm up at all when it's cold, and goddamn if it isn't just sweltering in the summer."

"Wasn't always that way," I said. The place he was describing sounded nothing like the cottage I knew. "When was the last time you were out there?"

"I go to check on it as regularly as I can but with the arthritis, feels like I'm tripping over every tree root. Remember how it was when we'd go up and fish? Lately though, it's just not the same. It's like an anchor around my neck."

"Dad. I'm a contractor. Why wouldn't you ask me for help?"

"You don't need this headache."

"I think I should have a look at it."

"Why bother?"

"If you're going to sell it, you're going to want to get the best price, right?" I said. "And it's what I do, Dad. Let me help."

My father shook his head and then shrugged. Gnarled fingers opened and closed stiffly and then finally rested on the table intertwined, his knuckles sticking out from his pale hands like tree roots trapped in concrete. "I don't know what you can do about it. I don't think anyone can do anything about it."

"Then there's no harm in John trying," Nadine said, reaching out to cover my father's hand with hers.

My dad jerked a little with the contact but he slowly turned his hand over to meet her palm to palm. Nadine smiled at my father. In those few moments he sat a little straighter. His eyes didn't seem so indelibly coloured with pain. I tried to imagine my parents sitting like this, hands clasped over a worry. Had they ever touched so easily, with so much comfort?

All day, those little moments when Nadine reached for me, those little signs that she was there, to calm me, to give strength, to buoy me up. I knew I didn't want to let her down, didn't want to disappoint her, didn't want her to feel as if she didn't matter. I didn't want her to feel betrayed as my mother had felt. I wasn't going to lose Nadine over something as silly as a lake cottage. Maybe this was the universe telling me something.

"I've got it, Dad. Let me see what I can do to get it ready for sale."

My father nodded still looking at Nadine. For the next hour, we nursed strong coffees, picked at sweet pastries and imbibed more easily digestible matters.

"You okay?" Nadine asked, when we got back into the car.

"Yeah. I'm fine."

"Maybe it's not as bad as he thinks."

"If he's got to sell the cottage, he's got to sell it. It's probably for the best."

Nadine leaned back in her seat and looked out the window as we resumed our trip. "Do you think your parents ever fought when they were dating?"

"That's a weird question."

"Maybe. But what do you think?"

"I never thought of my parents dating and they did so much fighting when they were married, I can't imagine them not."

"But logically, if they fought as much when they were dating, they probably would not have gotten married."

"Oh, we're using logic, now?" Nadine glared at me and I dropped my smugness like it was hot. "Pardon. Do go on."

"I bet they didn't fight at all."

"And that's a bad thing?"

"Yes. They were too afraid to ruin the relationship. So they pretended to be something they're not, to maintain it. There was something your mom said about the lake, about not troubling the waters."

"Yeah. I guess they just wanted things to go smoothly."

"And did they? They thought if they just pushed down their feelings, things would work themselves out. Until they couldn't help themselves anymore and all their resentment and disappointment came flooding up and the damn broke."

"So what are you saying?"

"I'm saying sometimes the only way to know yourself, the only way to let your partner know you, is to be really honest. That kind of honesty can be disturbing. Sometimes honesty means you have to trouble the waters."

I gripped the wheel and concentrated on the road. Hadn't I been honest with Nadine? And today couldn't have been more disturbing. As for my parents, they had fought over the cottage. But it wasn't going to be an issue with me and Nadine. My dad was selling it and there wasn't going to be any risk of that for us. I didn't have to worry about our marriage falling apart because I saw the cottage one way and she saw it another. Wasn't avoiding trouble a better way to go? So why wasn't I feeling better?

"We've reached a crossroads," I said. Nadine's head jerked up and she stared at me with concern. "I mean to say, we could go the long way to the cottage, where we've got road access. Or we go to the marina and grab our little skiff to take us across the lake."

Nadine smiled slowly. "After all this build-up, I want to see this infamous lake as quickly as possible."

I took the road to the left and in minutes, we drove into the marina. I slowed, rumbling down the gravel road to the docks and parked near the little grey skiff that bobbed forlornly on the water.

Mac came out to greet us, the grizzled sailor smiling though his straggled beard. "Your dad told me you were coming. Good to see you. And?"

"Mac, this is Nadine," I said as I began to unpack the car and load the boat.

"This one okay with taking the skiff? You been in a boat before, girl? You get too excited and you might find yourself in the water quicker than you think."

"Sort of like love," Nadine said.

"She's a fire-cracker, Johnny," Mac said as he walked away. "Make sure she don't set anything on fire."

Once out of the marina, I dangled my hand over the edge of the boat as I steered the motor. The water kissed my fingertips and I felt shivers dance across my skin. My heart beat in time with the thrum of the engine. I gripped the tiller hard, my arm clenched, bracing against the waves as if they were holding me back.

In the front of the boat, Nadine sat facing forward, leaning into the wind, as if she were as eager as I was. We cut across the bay and I aimed the skiff toward our shore. In the distance, I saw the grove of pine that signalled the beginning of the property.

"Hey," Nadine said, briefly turning to smile at me as she pointed ahead at the green tin roof of the cottage. "Is that it?"

I nodded.

When we got close enough, I cut the motor and we glided toward the dock.

"Before we unload, I'm going to have a look," I said tying onto the cleats. "We may end up heading back into town, if it's in too rough a shape."

Nadine nodded, her eyes wide and looking everywhere but at me. I was glad not to have her see my trepidation. I headed up toward the house, my footsteps suddenly lead, but before I went in, I turned to find her in the lake. She had kicked off her sandals and waded into water up to her knees. It was still clear enough to see her toes.

"Don't you find it cold?" I asked.

"Yeah, in a good way."

I looked past her to the lake. I wanted the water to ripple. I wanted something to rise up and look back at me long enough for Nadine to turn and see for herself. Did I need proof? Did I need justification? Justification for what?

"Be careful."

Nadine put her hands on her hips and tilted her head as she stared at me. "I'm not some little kid. I'm not going to drown. Nothing bad is going to happen." She frowned and stared down at the water. "Oh." Nadine brought one foot out of the water. She rested it on her knee to look at the heel. "My blister popped."

"Maybe you should put your shoes back on. I don't want that cut to get infected."

"Maybe you should relax." She released her foot and slid it back into the water. "It feels better than it has all day. Take a breath and go check things out."

I turned and walked toward the house, my eyes scanning the structure and the grounds, making a checklist; the loose and probably dangerously full eaves troughs, the rickety staircase, windows that could do with replacing. Nothing however seemed insurmountable, nothing felt dire, just the lack of loving attention.

I went to the shed to turn on the generator. It started without pause. I unlocked the front door and entered the cottage, heading toward the kitchen. Holding my breath, I turned on the faucet. Water flooded the sink, clear and odorless.

I felt someone behind me and turned to find Nadine standing in the doorway staring at me.

"Seems like your dad was worried about nothing. The pump is running fine. But he's right about that water. My blister already feels better. Do you know what people would pay to come out here and spend a week?"

"Really?"

"Sure. Don't let your parents' experience taint the possibilities."

I stared out the kitchen window. It looked out over the water. Again, I flashed back to the last time I remember my mother being at the lake. Her yelling from the end of the dock. Yelling out at the water. All in one motion, her arm cocked, and released, the wild motion carrying her around until she was facing away from the lake, to find me looking at her from the shore.

"Mom. Did you throw something in the lake?" I had asked. "You're not supposed to throw anything in the lake. It's not good for the water."

"Not good for the water," my mother had said. She took a breath and smoothed down the front of her shirt, tucking it back into her pants. "Don't be ridiculous. It's exactly what it wanted." She patted her hair back into place. "Now, get in the car with your brother."

I remember wondering what the lake could have wanted from my mother. But it wasn't about that. It was what she wanted. What Dad wanted. It was about how they had never been really honest. Not with themselves or each other. They had been too afraid to trouble the waters.

I felt Nadine close. Her head fell onto my shoulder as her arm wound around mine. Her grip tightened but it wasn't fear or panic. She just didn't want me to run. She held me in place, rooted me in the moment as I let my fears wash around me and through me.

"Nadine, I don't want my dad to sell the cottage. I want it."

Nadine looked up at me and captured me in her gaze. "Can you afford it?"

"I think so. I'll make it work. Work something out with my dad." I felt myself sinking, a stone thrown into a pool, water surrounding me. I let myself fall. I surrendered. "This place is important to me. I want you to know that."

"Good." Her arms slid around my neck and she stood on tiptoes her head resting on my shoulder.

My arms tightened around her. "Really? I was worried you wouldn't want to hear that."

"I was worried you wouldn't say it." She slid out of my arms but did not release me. She took me by the hand and led me toward a window in the dining area. "Did you know there's a structure back here?"

"No there's not."

"What do you call that?" she said, pointing through the window toward a clearing to the north of the house.

I squinted, trying to see past the bark and leaves, the pine blanketed ground. I am almost going to speak, to deny her hope, when I see one straight stiff unnatural line slightly raised but hidden among the bush. "I think you're right. I never knew that was there."

"Maybe the bad storms this spring cleared the area, but it's there now. And, Mr. Contractor, doesn't evidence of a previous structure mean we can build on it?"

"We?" I said, more to myself than to Nadine, who had already let herself out through the side door.

"Perfect place for a family or dining room," she yelled over her shoulder. "Don't you want to see what you can do with this place?"

"I take it we're staying," I said as I headed back to the dock.

I brought our things up from the boat. Nadine had already opened all the windows to air out the cottage and had started piling kindling in the woodstove. With one match, the fire caught, the smoke rising lazily up the stovepipe. I stepped outside to get a look at the chimney, backing up until I stood on the shore.

I heard a splash behind me. Something glimmered at the end of the dock; a pebble or a piece of shell or a shiny insect pausing to soak in the rays of the afternoon sun. But the more I stared at it, the closer I got, the more I knew that was not the case. I walked out slowly, balancing my weight to keep whatever was there from falling off the edge or through the slats and into the darkness and silt of the lake. The dock jiggled a little as I jerked in surprise. I held my breath and prayed the water still. There on the dock was my mother's ring surrounded by paw prints.

I eased down onto one knee and picked up the ring. I scanned the water. In the distance, a slight bump marred the perfect stillness of the lake and two glistening eyes stared back at me. I held out the ring. "Thanks." The bump sank below the lake.

"Nadine," I said, shifting to kneel in the direction of her approaching footsteps. "I have a question to ask you."

TO FIND A PEACH

FRANK SAVERIO

The streets of the Royal City were choked with death. At first, Cail had been nearly overpowered by the stench, a putrid mixture of decomposition and charred corpses. As he walked the streets, he was forced to cover his nose and mouth with a strip of cloth he tore from his cloak, though in truth, it did little good in keeping the foul taste of the city at bay.

I have seen battlefields far less terrible, he thought. At least those deaths were new, and the dark odor of blood and shit and fear was all a man had to contend with. Not this rotten, plague-ridden, lingering smoke that hung throughout the city.

That was something else that nagged at him as he strode through the nearly deserted streets. On the field of battle, the dead and dying were almost all men. Warriors who had more or less chosen to be there. In the houses and the alleyways of the Royal City, just as many of the corpses belong to women and children. The plague did not discriminate.

Beside him, Lande struggled to match Cail's long strides. The page's quick tapping footsteps barely registered as a counterpoint to the footfalls of his own solid boots.

I should have worn soft soles, he chided himself. The loud clunk of his hard heels announced their present to everyone within earshot. These days, most streets were quiet enough for those noises to bounce off the walls of houses and businesses and carry far. In the days before the plague, the bustle of these same streets would have made it impossible for him to even hear his own footsteps.

Cail let his hand fall to the pommel of his sword. The cold metal brought little comfort. He was a steward, not a warrior. His days as a fighter were long behind him, and none of them had been glorious, only steady and honorable. He supposed there was a quiet glory in that, but the days of having the luxury to reflect on such things were also long past.

"Do you see something, my lord?" Lande asked.

Cail glanced at him. The page had dropped his own hand onto the knife at his belt, miming Cail's action. The lad was only eleven, but he clearly dreamed of being a warrior. Perhaps he already saw himself as one.

Cail stopped in front of a shuttered shop. There were no red Xs painted on the wooden shutters. He wondered if that meant the merchant was still in business. The sign above the door was for a tailor, which did him no good. His princess had asked for a peach, and by the Unnamed, she would have it. Just not from a closed tailor's shop.

"My lord?"

Cail met the page's gaze. Lande was trying to affect a stern visage, but the trepidation he was feeling leaked out through his eyes like tears. Cail could see it there. He didn't blame him for it. If he was being honest, the same fears lurked somewhere inside of him. He was just better at keeping them from seeping out for all to see.

"What do *you* see, Lande?"

Lande's eyes widened slightly. "Me, lord?"

"You have eyes, don't you?"

"I do."

"Then use them. What do you see?"

Lande swallowed. His gaze swept the street and the buildings that lined it. Cail waited patiently. Lande was bright, even brighter than his previous page. When Gar was given his sword and sworn into royal service as a warrior, Cail had plucked Lande from the crowd of pages to serve him personally. Stewards to the royal house had a great many responsibilities, but one of those was ensure that the next generation of stewards were prepared for their role.

"The street looks empty," Lande told him. "But it's not."

"No, it isn't."

"I see a few people moving, in ones and twos. But they stay close to the walls of the buildings, and they hurry."

"They are afraid."

"Most of the businesses are closed," Lande continued. He pointed at the tavern halfway up the street. "But that one is still open."

Cail examined the tavern front. Behind the cloudy glass, he could see the figures Lande was pointing at. "And doing a brisk business, I imagine."

"But why?" Lande asked.

"What do you mean?"

Lande looked Cail in the eye. "We know that people catch the plague from other people. The sages are certain of it. That's how the queen died. The old king gave it to her. And she passed it on to both princes, before she knew she was infected."

"Shut up, boy," Cail growled. He glanced around to see if anyone might have heard Lande's words. He spotted a few of the shadowy figures well up the street that Lande had pointed out, making their way to whatever destination was important enough to risk the city streets. He didn't think any were close enough to hear the page's prattling.

He gave the boy a hard look. "Mind your tongue. The people can't know. Not yet."

Questions swarm in Lande's eyes, but he didn't ask them.

Cail leaned closer to him, speaking in a gruff whisper. "This city is in bad enough shape. Knowing the king and queen are still in the royal palace is the only thing keeping what little peace there is. Understand?"

Lande nodded, then looked down. "I'm sorry, my lord. I didn't think."

Cail put his hand on the boy's shoulder and squeezed. "It's all right, son."

Lande looked up at the word "son" and smiled. Cail tried to smile back, but knew his grizzled features probably conveyed something closer to a pained expression. It was the best he could do.

Despite his misstep in speaking aloud, Cail knew Lande had pointed out the biggest danger of this plague, as he saw it. No one knew right away that the infection had settled into their bones. By the time a person experienced the first fever, which usually preceded the black boils, he could have spread it to many others.

Or she.

Cail remembered when the queen had summoned him to her chamber, just over two weeks ago. She made him stand outside, speaking through a cracked door, while she lay in her bed, attended by a single handmaiden. Cail had seen others afflicted by the plague. Some experienced little pain, but for most, the black boils caused them agony. The king had roared almost until the end, as if he were facing a legion of his enemies on the battlefield. Only in his final moments did he fall silent. When Cail stood at the queen's door, listening to her panting breaths and grimaces, he could tell she was suffering dearly.

And yet, she uttered no complaints. No pleas for mercy. No pointless begging for a sage to offer treatment for what they could rarely cure, and then only in children. Instead, in short, staccato sentences, she asked after her sons.

"They show no signs," Cail had assured her.

"I touched them," she'd murmured through her tears. "I held them. I kissed their faces."

"They remain healthy, my queen."

"My sons," she moaned. "My beautiful sons."

Cail's own chest ached at the pain her voice. "They will stay beautiful, my queen. I will protect them."

She had laughed then. A short, barking, humorless laugh that ended in a phlegm-filled cough. "You are a liar, sir."

"My queen..."

"You are a liar, and may He bless you for it."

Cail had remained at her door for several minutes longer, but the queen had no more to say. Even so, she'd been right. Both boys were dead within a week, one right after the other. And Cail had been able to do nothing but watch them die.

"My lord?" Lande's high-pitched tones brought him back to the present.

"What?" He glanced down at Lande. "What else do you see?"

The page shrugged. "Just those few people moving from here to there. They're scared, like you said."

"Scared of us?"

"I don't think so. More scared of everything."

Cail grunted. He took a step down the alley that would take him to the street that lead to the food market, but Lande's voice stopped him.

"My lord, you didn't answer my question."

He turned to him. "I didn't?"

"No." Lande pointed to the tavern up the street. "If they know they can get the plague from other people, why go where there are people all around?"

Cail considered the question. The boy was only eleven. Then

again, if he was going to see all this death, he might as well know the truths of life. "When it feels like the world is ending, different men react differently. Some men try to fight it. Some seek out the sages and pray to Him, either for deliverance or for forgiveness, depending on the man. But some men...?" He jerked his head toward the tavern. "Some men decide that the best thing to do while you're waiting for the world to end is to get soundly drunk and find a woman."

Lande's eyes flared open. "You mean... not his wife?"

"I mean exactly that."

"I would never do that." Lande touched his heart and his forehead quickly with his fingertips, making the holy sign. "That goes against Him."

"So it does. But you asked." Cail turned and headed down the alley. "Now, come on."

Lande scampered to catch up. "Why do they—"

Cail held up his hand. "If you're going to ask me about men and women, don't. We'll talk about it when your voice changes."

Lande didn't answer, so Cail knew he'd been right about the question. They walked down the alleyway in silence. Ahead, off to their right, he could hear the crackling of a pyre, and the smell of burning death grew stronger.

When they emerged onto the street again, Cail turned left, heading up the gradual incline to the hilltop market. If any food merchants were still in business, it would be there. Those that hadn't fled the city, before the king ordered the gates sealed and held, would be faced with a hard decision. Selling their goods meant risking infection. For the craftsmen, closing the shop meant being unable to buy food for their families. For the food merchants, it meant watching their wares rot, though at least their own families would eat. For a while.

"My lord?"

Cail didn't reply. He kept walking up the slow rising street, his hand resting on his sword hilt.

Lande asked his question anyway, though he had the sense to keep his voice low. "Do you think they'll save the princess, my lord?'

"I do."

"But her brothers—"

Cail shot him a dark look.

Lande swallowed. "I meant to say, most people die from it."

"They do," Cail admitted. "But the sages caught her fever early, and that is the key. Or it seems to be."

Lande seemed to accept Cail's answer, and the boy fell silent as he half-ran beside him.

The taste of the oily smoke from the pyre they'd passed hung in the air. Cail spat, trying to clear it from his mouth. A few moments later, he heard Lande spit as well. He didn't need to glance over to know the boy's hand rested on his small knife, just as Cail's did on the hilt of his sword.

Why did I call him son? Cail mused. The last thing he needed was to feel that same terrible pain he'd gone through when Jerrel died. Or the two princes, for that matter. Better to keep the boy at an arm's length than to love him.

But he knew that was a lie as soon as he thought it. He had been a warrior once, out of duty, but he didn't have the cold bitterness of a warrior's heart. He loved too easily and too deeply, and he couldn't change that about himself any more than he could grow a third arm.

Maybe the boy would survive. Maybe they both would. Maybe the tumult and chaos of this plague would pass, and life would return to some semblance of normal again. The princess's recovery seemed likely. She was a sweet girl, and the people would eventually love her. She had men like him to do that hard work that came with ruling and advising. The Royal City might have been ravaged by the plague, but it would survive, and recover. Then they would retake the areas in the central region where the opportunistic heretics had rebelled, claiming that the plague was His holy wrath. Cail would gladly swing the sword again in battle if it meant bringing those traitors to justice.

But first they had to survive. *She* had to survive. Kara, the little princess. That last remaining child of King Olec. Once the plague was over and the bodies burned, and the people learned that their king and queen had fallen prey to the disease, and that the princes were gone as well, they would need her. She would hold the city, and all of Thesalia, together. Though a young girl, she had a spark in her soul, one that made everyone around her feel like family.

That morning, he'd visited her bedchamber, where she was

attended by a loyal handmaiden and Mattern, a sage who had risen to become the chief healer. Part of his ascent could be attributed to his skill, but Cail knew that wasn't the only reason. Even sages were not immune to the plague, and the ranks of their order had thinned as badly as any other.

Kara had seemed in high spirits. Mattern reported that she'd eaten her breakfast, and held down her food when he lanced and cleaned a boil that had appeared in the night. The viscous liquid was mostly clear, rather than the black ooze it ultimately evolved into, which Mattern assured him was another good sign.

"We must lance any boils before they turn black," Mattern said.

"Does it hurt, Princess?" Cail had asked her.

She smiled at him. "Only a little."

A pang of emotion hit Cail in the chest. So much rested on a nine-year-old girl. He wished he could protect her from all of it, but he knew he couldn't. It was her family's destiny to rule, and all he could do was help her when her turn came.

"You're very brave," he assured her. "You should have a reward for your bravery."

Her eyes lit up. "A peach, Lord Steward?"

Cail looked to Mattern for approval before he made a promise he might not be able to keep.

The sage gave him a nod. "The juices of the fruit will replenish her."

Cail turned back to the princess. "Then you shall have it."

He'd left her then, so that Mattern could continue to search her body for the beginnings of any other boils, and so she could rest.

The kitchens' stores were depleted. Agni, the cook, had died early on. She'd served three kings, but would not see a fourth. A thin apprentice named Hap had been promoted in her place. He didn't have Agni's skill when it came to cooking dishes, though his fare was satisfactory. But where his culinary abilities lacked, his organizational skills far exceeded his former mistress.

"We've enough for six months," he'd told Cail that morning. "Maybe a little more, maybe a little less. Depends on how you want me to ration it. And who dies between now and then."

When he'd asked about a peach, Hap had shaken his head. 'I've got some apples, though they're soft. There's still a few winter oranges from the west. But no peaches. Maybe in the market, Lord Steward."

Just a few hours later, he and Lande had ventured forth. The trip was as much to assess the city for himself as it was to find his princess a peach. He'd had reports from Larek, the veteran captain of the guard, who painted a picture of a subdued city, hunkered down to wait out the plague's run. Gar, his former page who patrolled the walls now, had a slightly different view of things. According to him, small gangs roamed the city, preying on the weak. The guard patrolled to prevent this, but they couldn't be everywhere at once. Cail wanted to see the situation for himself, and going to the hilltop market provided the perfect reason.

They came upon the first fruit stand halfway up the hill. It had abandoned by its owner, and what few pieces of fruit remained on the cart had turned so black that Cail couldn't recognize what they'd been.

Lande wrinkled his nose. "Stinks."

"You're just now noticing the smell?"

"I mean the fruit. Sweet stink is the worst."

Cail didn't answer, but he didn't agree with what the boy said. He'd already smelled the worst stench, and the strip of cloth across his face did nothing to keep it out. "Keep looking."

Lande made a face but returned to the cart.

"What are we looking for here?" The smooth voice came from behind them, and Cail heard the danger in it immediately. He whirled around to face the sound.

A tall, slender man in dark brown clothing emerged from the alleyway. Cail glanced down to the man's waist, where he wore a long dagger on each hip. Two more men stepped out of the narrow alley and into the street. One was short and wiry, the other a bit taller and stockier. Both held cudgels.

"Stand away," Cail ordered. "We are on royal business."

The man smiled darkly. "Royal business, is it? Has the good king sent his men out to raid my fruit cart? Things in the palace must be dire indeed."

Cail sensed Lande standing beside him, but he kept his eyes fixed on the tall man who spoke. "Your cart?"

"Yes, mine."

"You don't look like a fruit monger."

"And you don't look like a thief."

"That's because I'm not."

The man chuckled, his tone sarcastic. "What would you call rooting around in someone else's property, intending on taking whatever you find? Because that sounds a lot like stealing to me."

"Who are you?" Cail asked.

"Who asks?"

Cail hesitated for a moment, but decided to tell the truth. Perhaps his title would change their intentions. "I am Cail Auger, Lord Steward to King Olec. Who are you?"

The man's eyes widened slightly when Cail spoke, but otherwise, he did not react. "I am called Silk."

"I am on royal business, Silk, and you will stand away!"

Silk smiled. "That's the second time you've given me an order. Will there be a third?"

"Does there need to be?"

Silk shrugged. "I suppose not. I'll ask you the obvious question, then." He leaned forward and raised his eyebrows. "Stand away... *or what?*"

Cail tore his sword from its sheath, but Silk was even quicker to draw his long daggers. The man lunged toward Cail, driving both blades at him. Cail stepped to the side to avoid the low blow and parried high to block the other. Silk grinned evilly at him.

"Let's play, old man," he said, his tone mocking. He twirled both knives, moving them in a crisscrossing pattern in front of him. "I've always wanted to carve something royal. You're not part of the royal family, but you'll have to do."

Cail brought his sword into a ready position, and waited.

"Oh, that won't be enough," Silk said. "I assure you." His evil smile brimmed with self-confidence.

Then he screamed. "You little *bastard!*" He whirled around on Lande, causing the boy to lose his grip on his small dagger. He had buried it to the hilt in Silk's thigh. His two henchman stood frozen, gaping at their leader in surprise.

Silk slashed out at Lande, catching him across the cheek. The boy cried out and toppled to the ground.

Before Silk could follow Lande to the ground with his blades, Cail stepped forward and drove his sword through the small of the man's back. Silk let out a muted scream that dissolved into a wet gasp. His arms flopped uselessly to his sides, both knives tumbling from his slack fingers to the ground.

Cail jerked back on his sword, but it didn't budge. His blade was caught. He pulled again, but couldn't dislodge it. In desperation, he planted his foot against Silk's buttocks and pulled back while pushing forward with his boot. The blade wrenched free, and he staggered back several steps.

The cudgel blow caught him on the left shoulder a moment later. White pain shot down his arm and into his chest. He let out a cry and spun away. The next swing of the cudgel whistled past his ear as he turned.

Cail let his momentum drive him as he finished the spin with a blind swing of the blade. He aimed for where he thought the man would be, and he wasn't far off. The edge of his sword cut deeply into the back of the stocky man's legs. The attacker fell to the ground, screaming. Blood pooled around him as he writhed on the stones of the street, clutching at his wounds.

He was finished.

Cail wheeled around to find the final enemy. He didn't have to look far. The short, wiry man held Lande by the hair, his cudgel raised in the air.

"Don't come any closer!" he screamed.

Cail watched him for a long moment, then took one careful step toward them.

The man gave Lande a jerk, making the boy gasp. "I'll bash his brains in, old man," he promised.

Cail took another step. He dropped his gaze to meet Lande's. A ribbon of blood ran from the cut on his cheek. The boy's eyes were scared, but not panicked.

"Stop, I said!"

"No," Cail answered, taking another step. "You won't hurt him."

"You don't think I have the guts to do it, old man?" the man sneered, though Cail could hear the fear in the man's voice. Silk must have been the leader of this trio, and this man the consummate follower.

"No," Cail said. He moved forward again. "You would do it. If you could."

The man's eyes hardened and he raised his cudgel in the air to strike Lande.

Cail strode forward rapidly, taking the final two steps to reach him. His blade arced through the air, slicing into the main's arm just below the elbow. The hand and the cudgel dropped harmlessly to the ground. The wiry man stared in disbelief at the bleeding stump of his arm. He barely seemed to register it when Lande tore away from him.

Cail raised his foot and drove a kick into the man's midsection. The man flew backward, flopping onto the street. Then the street fell quiet once again, with only the low moans of the dying.

Cail didn't wait to see any more. He turned to find Lande; but it was Lande who found him. The boy vaulted toward Cail, wrapping his arms around him. Cail returned the embrace, squeezing him tightly. After a few moments, he took Lande by the upper arms and moved him back to look at his face.

The cut from the crest of his cheekbone nearly to his mouth, but it hadn't cut deeply enough to go through. Lande reached up and touched it gingerly. "It's not bad, is it?"

"It's not good, but you'll live." Cail gave him a hint of a smile so that the boy knew he'd been joking.

Cail retrieved Lande's dagger from Silk's thigh, wiping the blood on the dead man's shirt. Then he carefully sliced a strip and then a square from his already ruined cloak. He folded over the square and pressed it against Lande's cheek so that the wound was covered. "Hold that," he directed the boy.

While Lande pressed the cloth against the wound, Cail used the strip he'd cut to tie it in place. He tried several different ways before he found one that worked, wrapping the strip horizontally around the boy's head with the knot below his nose.

"It'll double as something to keep the stench out," he told him.

"It hurts," Lande said, his voice sounding like he had a cold.

"It's a cut."

"No, the knot. It's tight."

"Leave it. We'll get something better when we get back to the palace." He looked closely at Lande, wondering if he should take the boy back directly. He could return later for the peach.

Lande seemed to sense his thoughts. "I'll be fine," he assured him. "Really."

Cail considered, but decided to finish what they'd started. The market center wasn't far now, and he didn't want to return empty-handed.

"All right," he said. "But if you feel dizzy or sick, you tell me."

"I will."

Cail looked at him for a moment longer, then squeezed his shoulder. "I almost lost you there, son."

Lande smiled despite the bandage. "You were incredible, lord. The way you swung your sword. I've never seen—"

"You've never someone who can truly wield a blade, or you wouldn't be so impressed," Cail finished.

"No, lord. You were very good. You—"

"I almost got us killed by not paying attention. Let that be a lesson to you of what not to do. Now, let's go."

They continued up the hill. Most of the shops were closed. Cail heard the rhythmic clank of a blacksmith working long before they passed his shop. He took some comfort in the familiar sound. At least some men chose to defy the plague.

They gave a wide berth to the meat shop, though Cail saw a gaunt butcher standing at the counter inside. Only a few dark items hung from the ceiling, and he didn't like the smell of the place.

Cail stopped at a pair of rival flower carts right next to each other. Many of the small bouquets looked fresh. A young girl manned the first stand, an elderly woman the second.

"I'm looking for peaches," Cail said. "Do you know if any of merchants have peaches?"

The young girl shrugged and pointed at a wreath of daisies. Her eyes were vacant, and Cail recognized the expression. The petals of the praying tulip were edible. It was said that the tulip prayed to forget, and those who ate its petals forgot as well.

"She's a fool," the old woman snapped. "Young and beautiful and a fool."

Cail looked over the old woman's wares. They were in no better shape than the girl's. He looked up at the woman. "You own both carts?"

"What a stupid question. Of course I do."

"You're speaking to the Lord Steward!" Lande told her shrilly, though the bandage made him sound strange.

The woman's expression betrayed no surprise. She scowled at Lande. "And you're speaking to your elder, so mind your tongue, boy. Or is that how you got your cut there?"

Lande blanched under her gaze. He flicked his eyes toward Cail for a moment, but remained silent.

"Peaches?" Cail asked again. "Do you know anyone selling them?"

The old woman swept her open hand over her flowers. "Perhaps if the Lord Steward were to honor an old woman with his patronage?"

Cail considered. Then he reached inside his shirt pocket for a silver coin. "Lande," he said, "pick a nice bouquet for the queen. She loves flowers at her dinner table."

Lande cleared his throat. "Yes, my lord." He took a long while before selecting a tiny bunch of white and pink buttercups.

Cail handed the old woman a coin. She took his from his fingers and hid it away.

"Randal," she said. "He always has the best peaches."

"He's still open?" Cail asked.

"Last I saw."

"When was that?"

"Yesterday afternoon. He bought some praying tulips for his wife on his way down the hill."

"Which shop is his?"

"You'll find it," she said. "There aren't many open."

Cail handed her a second coin. "By His mercy," he said.

"May He protect you."

He and Lande turned and headed back up the hill.

Empty shops and abandoned stalls flanked their way. Two of the shops were shuttered closed with red Xs slashed across the doorways.

Another was burned nearly to the ground, a few black timbers the only skeletal remains.

What has happened to our beautiful city? Cail wondered if the heretics from the central region were right, and it was His wrath, punishing them for their sins. But what sins?

He smiled grimly. He supposed there was more than enough sin to choose from, if one were looking for reasons for Him to be angry with Thesalia and its people. All of the holy claims and surface rituals didn't hide the acts that happened in dark places, and behind closed doors. He saw it all, in His glory.

Or so Cail was told.

They crested the rise to the flat hilltop that was the central market. In times past, the market bustled with activity and so thick with people almost shoulder to shoulder. Today, he saw a lone woodcutter, splitting and stacking on the far side of the square. All of the stalls stood empty. Small tendrils of smoke rose from another blacksmith's shop, but Cail could hear no activity within.

"That's it!" Lande said excitedly, pointing. "Over there!"

Cail looked. The grocer's shop sat at the opposite end of the square from the woodcutter. Even from where they were, he could see that door stood open.

"Come on!" Lande cried, his voice ringing with excitement. He took a step, starting to run.

Cail grabbed hold of the boy's arm roughly, jerking him back. "Wait," he said. "We stay together." He released Lande's arm.

The boy rubbed where he'd grabbed, his expression hurt.

"Stick to my side," Cail commanded. "Understand?"

Lande nodded sullenly.

Cail started across the square, his eyes sweeping left and right for any threat. There had been reports of crowds gathering earlier in the week. Angry crowds, he'd been told, though he imagined some were simply hungry. But there was little sign of anyone moving in the square, aside from the rhythmic whack and pause of the woodcutter's work.

As he neared the doorway to the shop, Cail tried to peer inside. The overcast sky gave as little light as it did warmth, and he could only see a few indistinct shadows. As best he could tell, they were shelves and tables.

What did you expect in a grocery merchant's shop?

"Stay close to me," he muttered to Lande, then stepped inside. It took a few moments for his eyes to adjust to the dimness. A rustle of movement near the back of shop drew his eyes toward the sound. Before he could make out the shape, a match flared, briefly illuminating a lumpy man holding an unlit lamp.

"Welcome, friends," the man said, and used the match to ignite the lamp. A weak light filled the interior of the shop. The merchant held it out high at an arm's length in their direction.

Cail looked around for anyone else, but saw no one.

"Are you Randal?"

"I am. And this is my shop." He swept his free hand across the room, then dropped it. "What's left of it, anyway."

"Most of the others are closed," Cail said.

"True. Most of them have either died, or their family has died. A few were smart enough to close sooner. Smarter than me. They stay away now to protect their families."

"But you're open."

Randal smiled humorlessly. "We all must do our part..."

"For the greater good of all," Cail said, finishing the popular aphorism from His word.

"Yes," Randal agreed. "Only I wish I were truly so unselfish. The truth is, I have no family. Not anymore. My son is gone, and my wife stares into the cold ashes of our fireplace with vacant eyes."

"Why aren't you with her?"

Randal shrugged. "She's not really there. And if I don't sell what I have in stock, it will rot. Then we'll both starve."

"You don't fear the plague?" Lande asked him.

Cail shushed him, but Randal shook his head and answered. "Death is death, boy. We all find it eventually, no matter how hard we may think we will not." He peered a little closer at Lande. "You look a little like my own boy, even with that bandage. Paul, he was called."

"An old name," Cail observed.

"Unlike my son," Randal said. "The plague claimed him." He gave Cail an appraising look. "You, I know, I think."

"Perhaps."

"You are the Lord Steward to the King. Or whoever is still living in that palace, anyway."

"I am," Cail said.

"What profound mission brings you to my humble shop?" Randal said, smiling at his own soft sarcasm. "Will there be a royal feast that I can supply?"

"Nothing so grand, I'm afraid."

"No?" Randal looked disappointed. "Then what?"

"I'm surveying the state of our city," Cail said. "But when I saw your shop was open, I thought I might stop in for a peach."

"A peach?"

"Yes. The princess is fond of them."

Randal nodded slowly. He shuffled to a bin near Cail and held the lamp above it. "Most of my fruit has begun to rot, my lord Steward. But you are welcome to search while I hold the light for you. There may be a peach or two, though I doubt it."

Cail stepped forward, watching Randal's eyes. The merchant met his gaze without any sign of subterfuge, but that didn't convince him. Many men were skilled at hiding behind masks of their own creation.

"Lande," he said, continuing to watch Randal as he spoke. "Look in the bin."

The boy scrambled forward, immediately bending over the edge of the bin and scanning the fruit. "It's mostly bad," he said.

"My apologies," Randal said.

"It stinks, too."

"True enough, I'm afraid."

Cail waited while Lande moved pieces of fruit from one side to the other, searching diligently. The longer the boy took, the more impatient Cail could feel himself becoming. He almost joined in the search, but the shopkeeper's watchful nature worried him, so he waited.

"I've got one!" Lande cried out. He stood suddenly, holding up his hand in triumph. His face beamed with pride.

Cail examined his find. The peach was small, and slightly wizened. The wrinkles made it look as if it had grown elderly. A blackened patch the size of his fingernail adorned the side.

I can cut that away. This will work.

"Nicely done, lad," he said gruffly, and turned his eye back to Randal. "What do I owe you?"

Randal smiled. "A peach for our beautiful princess? In the midst of all this death and fire? Now, that is worth quite a lot, wouldn't you say?"

"You won't chisel me, merchant. How much? And make it a fair price."

"Prices in this city aren't what they used to be." Randal shook his head mournfully.

"Swords are." Cail dropped his hand onto his pommel.

Randal's eyes flared in surprise, and he raised his hands to placate him. "You mistake me, lord. I was indulging in mere bit of sad philosophy, that is all. I meant no affront."

"A philosopher merchant, huh?"

Randal shrugged. "When you see as many people as I have, for as long as I have, it is inevitable. Wouldn't you say?"

"I'd say leave it to the sages. How much for the peach?"

Randal's eyes flicked to the peach, which Lande still held up in the air like a prize. "It's priceless," he said, his eyes seemingly far away for a moment. Then his focus returned and he glanced back to Cail. "So it shall have no price. It will be a gift for the princess."

"A gift?" Cail peered at him, confused. A few moments ago, the merchant sounded like he was trying to gouge Cail for his entire money pouch. Now he wanted to give his wares away?

"Wait here," Randal said. He shuffled to the back of the store and returned with a small patch of burlap. When he reached out to take the wrinkly, decrepit peach from Lande, the boy pulled his hand away.

"Give it to him," Cail instructed.

Reluctantly, Lande extended his hand toward Randal, his expression suspicious. The merchant took the peach and wrapped it in the burlap, tying it shut with a bit a string. Then he handed it back to Lande.

"That should keep it safe until you reach the princess," he said.

"Thank you," Cail said. He reached for his pouch, but Randal shook his head and waved his hands.

"No, I meant what I said, my lord Steward. Keep your coin."

Cail studied him a few moments longer, then nodded. "I'll tell her from where it came," he promised.

"That is enough." Randal pulled the lamp closer to his own face, revealing a pair of small black boils on his neck, just above his collar. "It will be a comfort in the days to come."

Cail understood then. "I'm sorry," he whispered.

Randal waved away his sympathy. "It is better that I join them, if that is what awaits us."

"I pray it is," Cail said.

"We all do."

"By His mercy, then."

"May He protect you," Randal replied. "Though He protected no one here."

Cail backed away, watching Randal, but the merchant did not move. He only stared back, his eyes sad and resigned.

"Come on, Lande," Cail said quietly, still walking backward. "Let's go."

Lande followed him out the open door. Only once he'd cleared the threshold did Cail turn around.

"You have the peach?"

Lande help up the burlap bag.

"Then let's get home."

The walk back down the hill was easier than the walk up. He gave a nod to the old woman at the flower cart as they passed. She nodded back, but the young woman next to her only stared at them blankly.

When they reached the scene of the earlier fight, all three men lay still, each in pool of their own blood. Cail made Lande give them a wide berth anyway. Once they were past, Cail hurried him along, watching for other street bandits.

They kept up a brisk pace. Cail swiveled his head back and forth, forward and back, but he saw nothing other than a few creeping souls. Their movements reminded him of the way the two boils on Randal's neck crept out from beneath his shirt.

By the time they reached the palace gate, Cail's jaw was sore from clenching it.

"Lord Steward," the sergeant of the guard acknowledged him, then swung open the gate.

Once the gate was closed behind them, Cail allowed himself to relax. He held out his hand to Lande. "The peach," he said. "And the bouquet."

Lande looked hurt. "I'd... I'd hoped to give it to her, my lord."

Cail shook his head. "The sages won't let but a few people near her. At least until the treatments run their course."

Lande hung his head, but he handed over the items.

"Go see Hap in the kitchens," Cail told him. "Get some stew and some bread in you. I'll come get you after, and we'll finish cleaning up that wound of yours."

"Yes, my lord." Lande's tone was crestfallen.

Cail put his hand on the boy's shoulder. "You'll carry that scar for the rest of your life, son. Let it remind you of the day you became a warrior."

Lande's eyes brightened at that. "Yes, lord."

"Now, go. And tell Hap I sent you."

Lande scampered off toward the kitchen. Cail watched him go. He wasn't Jerrel. He would never be Jerrel. But he was something. Something... good. And that was more than he thought he'd ever have again, outside of the royal family.

He made his way up the stairs to the royal apartments, letting the peach sway little in its little bag. Around the corner from the princess's chamber, he stopped and opened it so he could carve out the blackness. He cut deeper than he needed to, flicking away some good flesh along with the rotted bit, but it was better to be cautious with these things.

Cail stared down at the pitiful piece of fruit. The peach seemed shrunken in on itself, as if aged. The hole where he'd excised the blackness looked like a wound. But despite that, he could smell the light odor of the peach. It smelled good to him. It smelled clean.

Carefully, he re-wrapped the burlap and tied it shut. All good presents should be presented thusly. He imagined what Kara's eyes would look like when she saw the peach, and when she ate it. That joy made the trip worth the cost. He regretted not bringing Lande along to see it, too. The boy had certainly earned it, in blood.

He rounded the corner and approached the door. The royal guard that stood watch recognized him right away. He stepped forward, then stopped.

"My lord…"

"What is it?"

"I'm… I'm to not allow anyone inside."

"Why?"

"The sage. He ordered it."

Cail swallowed hard. "When?"

"Half hour ago, lord."

Cail nodded, his heart sinking. "All right. Thank you." He stepped forward, reaching for the door. The guard seemed to consider stopping him, but didn't.

When he stepped through the door, Mattern the sage looked up sharply. His expression softened when he saw Cail. He stood and walked to him. "My lord, she's gone. I'm sorry."

"No." Cail shook his head. "She was responding to the treatments. She was getting better."

Mattern pressed his lips together and nodded in sympathy. "I know. But sometimes…" He trailed off, then began again. "There was nothing more I could do. She passed quickly."

Cail brushed past him. At the bedside, he looked down at Princess Kara. He'd hoped her face would appear peaceful, that he could take solace in that. But her features were slack and lifeless, no more.

Cail put the burlap-clad peach into her loose fingers, wrapping them around the gift. If he'd been faster, perhaps she could have tasted the peach before she died. She could have had that, at least.

"She was the last of her family," Mattern said from behind him. "What will we do now?"

Cail set the small bouquet beside her, and stared down at the little girl who had once been so beautiful, so full of life.

"We carry on," he said, his voice thick with tears. "Like always."

Mattern was silent for a while. Cail stroked Kara's hair, remembering the magical moments when the little princess had smiled. Her loving nature made him feel as if he were family, and she shared that smile widely. She would have been a good queen, he believed, one the people would have loved. Early on, she'd have relied on her advisors to help her understand statecraft, but even as a young girl, she already understood people.

"How?" Mattern's voice cracked with uncharacteristic emotion. "The family is dead."

Cail shook his head. "Not the whole family."

"Distant cousins remain, certainly," Mattern chuffed. "But they're few, and scattered across the realm. Besides, none is any more worthy than you or I."

Cail looked up from the still figure before him. "Worthy?"

"Of the blood," Mattern clarified. "Part of the true family. Descended."

"There is an answer," Cail insisted. "And it is men like you and I that must find it."

"Are you suggesting...?" The sage trailed off, the idea sinking in.

"Our city needs us. Our nation needs us."

"Our nation needs the royal family. And they are gone."

"They are." Cail swallowed past the lump in his throat. "Did you love them, sage?"

Mattern nodded. "I did, truly."

"And the king and his family loved our people," Cail responded. "So our duty is clear."

"We're not of the blood." Mattern's protest sounded rote to him, but he knew it was one had to overcome.

"No," Cail admitted. "But we are here. We are alive. And we have to do what we can. For those that have died." His gaze flicked to the princess, then back to Mattern. "And for all those who yet live."

Like Lande, he thought.

"But...rule?"

"For a time, yes."

Mattern stared at him long and hard. Weariness and realization were etched in equal parts in his grizzled features. Finally, nodded his agreement. "If we must."

Cail didn't answer. He knew what he had to do. And regardless of everything, he knew the one terrible truth that always remained.

Tomorrow would come. There was work to be done. And they would endure.

THANK YOU!

Tell the world what you thought of *The Wand that Rocks the Cradle*—leave a reader review on Amazon. Thank you so much!

Sign up to the Lagrange Books mailing list for periodic news on our newest projects! You can even join our Advance Reader Team, giving you the opportunity to read new books for free in exchange for your honest reviews on Amazon and other online marketplaces. Find us at: orenlitwin.com/lagrangebooks.

ABOUT THE AUTHORS

Misha Burnett has been writing poetry and fiction for around forty years. During this time he has supported himself and his family with a variety of jobs, including locksmith, cab driver, and building maintenance. His first four novels, *Catskinner's Book*, *Cannibal Hearts*, *The Worms Of Heaven*, and *Gingerbread Wolves* comprise a series, "The Book Of Lost Doors." Major influences include Tim Powers, Samuel Delany, William Burroughs, and Phillip K. Dick.

Misha's short story "In the City of Dreadful Joy" recently won third place in the 2019 Baen Adventure Fantasy Award. That story and the other Erik Rugar casefiles will soon be published by Lagrange Books!

Marion Deeds lives in northern coastal California, which is the most beautiful place in the world, and she's not biased at all. (She's willing to admit that Iceland is a close second.) Her short fiction has been published in *Podcastle*, *Daily Science Fiction*, *Flash Fiction Online*, and in the anthologies *Strange California* and *Beyond the Stars, Unimagined Realms*. She's a conventional storyteller in an experimental world, someone who loves to walk, read, daydream, watch squirrels and feed the local crows. Catch up with her on Twitter: @mariond_d.

Michelle F Goddard is a musician who has performed around the world, and a composer with credits to her name for songs in musicals and films. Her short fiction has been published in Reality Skimming Press's *Water* anthology, and Iguana Books' *Blood is Thicker* anthology with more publications forthcoming. She is presently working on several short stories and a Science Fiction novel.

Elana Gomel was born in a country that no longer exists and has visited every continent but Africa and Antarctica. In addition to being a cosmopolitan and a part-time fantasy and science fiction writer, she is a full-time academic focusing on narrative theory. Elana is an Associate Professor at the Department of English and American Studies, Tel-Aviv University, and has been a Visiting Scholar at Princeton, Stanford, and University of Hong Kong.

W.O. Hemsath loves writing anything with a speculative twist and believes the everyday world holds a little magic for anyone willing to look for it. She has a B.A. in Screenwriting from Chapman University, has sold and/or published multiple flash fiction and short story pieces, and is currently revising a YA sci-fi novel. Her secret love is writing song parodies, and there is precious little she won't do in this world for a good back scratch or brownie a la mode. While she has lived on three different continents (and traveled to two others), she currently resides in Minnesota with her husband and four sons.

Joanna Hoyt lives with her family on a Catholic Worker farm in upstate New York where she spends her days tending goats, gardens and guests and her evenings reading and writing stories. She has been part of a church group that did outreach to migrant workers and offered hospitality to those who were injured. Her stories have recently appeared in publications including Factor Four Fiction, Metapsychosis, and Upper Rubber Boot Books' anthology *Broad Knowledge: 35 Women Up To No Good*.

Frank Saverio grew up reading the likes of Piers Anthony, J.R.R. Tolkien, and Stephen R. Donaldson. He lives in central Oregon with his wife, where he is working on his first fantasy novel. He has also written more than two dozen crime fiction novels under the name Frank Zafiro.

P.L. Sundeson is a native New Orleanian who hates the climate and the parades, yet still draws inspiration from the city. He has done time as a delivery driver, radio announcer/producer, and computer programmer/analyst/technical writer, and since 2002 has worked as an administrator for Tulane University. His short stories have appeared in online magazines Crime and Suspense, Thrilling Detective, Mysterical-E, and Under the Rainbow. In February 2019 his short story "One Summer Night, With Spirits" won first place in the inaugural New Orleans Public Library Winter Writing Contest.

www.ingramcontent.com/pod-product-compliance
Lightning Source LLC
Chambersburg PA
CBHW030231180626
46810CB00008B/3068